Renee closed the door and paced her small living room

She twisted her hands in agitation, not quite sure what she'd hoped would happen just now, but definitely disappointed that nothing at all had happened.

Yet the very fact that she'd looked into his eyes and felt a tingle zing from her stomach to her feminine parts made her extremely wary. She wasn't supposed to be attracted to John Murphy. The man had complicated her life in a way that should make him Public Enemy #1 in her eyes, but she was slowly seeing him in a different light.

And that was not good. Better to keep the battle lines firmly drawn. They were not on the same side. They were simply being civil to one another for the sake of the kids.

Dear Reader,

Somehow we expect mothers to always know what the right decision is, and when they fail—as most humans are wont to do—we judge them harshly. Since becoming a mother myself I've discovered that we learn as we go and sometimes the lessons are painful and the learning curve steep.

Renee Dolling is a woman who in the past has made some serious mistakes that have affected her children in a detrimental way. Making amends isn't as easy as saying "I'm sorry," and gaining forgiveness is nearly impossible when you can't forgive yourself. That's where Renee is when she meets John Murphy, a reclusive horse trainer who relates better to animals than people.

It's not love at first sight. In fact, Renee is as approachable as a hissing cat and John doesn't feel the need or the desire to find out why she's so defensive and prickly. Fortunately, there are three little girls to bring them together when neither seems amenable to even being civil to one another. Sharing a love for the girls inevitably opens their eyes to each other and a new future together.

Hearing from readers is one of my greatest joys (aside from really good chocolate), so don't be shy. Feel free to drop me a line at my Web site, www.kimberlyvanmeter.com, or through snail mail at P.O. Box 2210, Oakdale, CA 95361.

Happy reading,

Kimberly Van Meter

KIDS ON THE DOORSTEP
Kimberly Van Meter

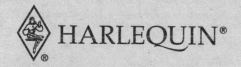

TORONTO • NEW YORK • LONDON
AMSTERDAM • PARIS • SYDNEY • HAMBURG
STOCKHOLM • ATHENS • TOKYO • MILAN • MADRID
PRAGUE • WARSAW • BUDAPEST • AUCKLAND

Recycling programs
for this product may
not exist in your area.

ISBN-13: 978-0-373-71577-0

KIDS ON THE DOORSTEP

ABOUT THE AUTHOR

An avid reader since before she can remember, Kimberly Van Meter started her writing career at sixteen when she finished her first novel, typing late nights and early mornings on her mother's old portable typewriter. Although that first novel was nothing short of literary mud, with each successive piece of work her writing improved to the point of reaching that coveted published status.

Kimberly, now a journalist, and her husband and three kids make their home in Oakdale. She enjoys writing, reading, photography and drinking hot chocolate by the windowsill when it rains.

Books by Kimberly Van Meter

HARLEQUIN SUPERROMANCE
1391—THE TRUTH ABOUT FAMILY
1433—FATHER MATERIAL*
1469—RETURN TO EMMETT'S MILL*
1485—A KISS TO REMEMBER*
1513—AN IMPERFECT MATCH*

*Emmett's Mill stories

To the mothers of the world: raising children is the most important job we as adults will ever have, as they are our legacy and our future.

To my sister, Kristen, who wears the badge of motherhood with pride and inspires people to love without reservation, without judgment, without fear. She is a mama bear and a wonder to watch in action!

CHAPTER ONE

JOHN MURPHY HAD JUST STOKED the fire and returned to his well-worn leather chair with his newspaper in hand when an urgent knock at the front door had him twisting in surprise.

It was nearly ten o'clock at night and the rain was quickly turning to sleet. This storm was supposed to hit the California Sierra Nevadas pretty hard by dumping a load of snow in the high country and plenty of it even in the foothills, so anyone with any kind of sense knew better than to be out and about. A bad feeling settled in his gut. There was no one he could imagine who would venture into this storm without good reason.

"John? It's me, Gladys."

The sound of his neighbor's voice, thin and reedy, alarmed him. It was too late for house calls of an ordinary nature and Gladys—after going through surgery a few days prior—should've been in bed resting.

He opened the door and Gladys offered him a weak and somewhat pained smile as she and three little girls were ushered in from the biting cold.

"What the hell is going on?" he asked yet immediately guided Gladys to his leather chair. "What in the Sam Hill are you doing out in this storm in your condition? You just had surgery, woman. Are you trying to kill yourself?"

"Don't yell at her. It's not her fault," piped up the middle girl whose short stack of wild hair was matted to her head. The poor kid looked like a drowned pixie. She rubbed at her pert nose but stared John down with attitude. "Daddy didn't stay long enough to listen that she was sick."

John ran his hand through his hair. "And you are? And who's your daddy?"

"We're the Dollings and I'm Taylor," the little tyke proclaimed, ignoring the nervous jostling from her older sister to be quiet. "Who are you?" she asked without hesitation.

"John Murphy," he grunted in answer. "And your daddy?"

Gladys broke in with a grimace. "This is Alexis, Taylor and the little one is Chloe. Oh, John, it's the most deplorable situation and I didn't know what to do. Look at them, the poor chickpeas, they're practically frozen to the bone and wearing nothing more than rags. I could throttle that irresponsible boy for this!"

"Throttle who?" John was growing more perplexed by the moment, but Gladys was obviously distressed enough without his blustering adding to it so he tried for patience. "Tell me what's going on here."

Gladys compressed her lips to a fine line. "My sister's grandson, Jason, God rest her soul that she never saw how badly he turned out, just showed up on my doorstep with the girls, saying he couldn't handle it anymore and he needed me to keep them for a while until he got back on his feet. More likely so that he can be footloose and fancy-free, is what I think but before I could talk some sense into him, he was gone." Her gaze softened as she took in the children's forlorn appearance but when she turned to him again, her expression was full of worry and embarrassment. "I didn't know what to do. I don't want to take them to the authorities. They are my family, even if only distantly."

The littlest, she couldn't be more than three he wagered, sneezed and he realized they were still standing there soaked. He went to the hall closet and returned with three blankets. Giving one to each girl, he told them to warm up by the fire while he tried making sense of things with Gladys.

"Start from the beginning," he instructed in a low voice so as not to scare the kids. "Where is their father and when is he coming back? Or how about their mother for that matter? They have to have a mother somewhere."

"Daddy said Mommy left us," Taylor answered before Gladys could. John turned toward Taylor and she continued, bundled in the blanket, despite several attempts by her older sister to shush her. She glowered at her sister. "Well, that's what he said."

"It's no one's business," the older one said, adding in a low tone, "Especially no stranger."

John looked to Gladys. "He split? No number, nothing?"

"Nothing. He barely took time enough to push the girls out of the car with their bag and then was off again. I tried to stop him but he was too fast for me." That last part came out accompanied by a trembling lip and John knew Gladys was ashamed of her weakened state. Under normal circumstances the older woman was like a hurricane but the last year had been rough on her and her age was starting to slow her down. He patted her knee in some semblance of comfort but he was certainly caught in a bad spot. It was clear Gladys was loath to involve the authorities but she wasn't in any shape to care for the kids herself.

John eyed the older girl. "Alexis, right? I take it you're the oldest?" She nodded warily. "How old are you?" he asked.

Alexis raised her chin. "I'm nine, almost ten. Taylor is five and Chloe is three."

So incredibly young. Essentially abandoned. John was at a loss of what to do. The closest he'd ever come to babies or children were his nephews and they only visited on holidays. Frankly, he was about as equipped to deal with these kids as a dog was to teach a cat how to fetch. But he knew he couldn't very well toss them out on their ears. Gladys had come to him for help even though the old girl was a little addled if she thought he was her best option. The girls stared up at him, waiting, and he realized he couldn't just stand there scratching his head.

"You need to get out of those wet clothes. If you don't already have pneumonia, you will by tomorrow," he grumbled, wondering what he could possibly find to fit three little girls. "And then, I think we ought to call Sheriff Casey, she'll know what to do for you guys."

"We're girls," Taylor corrected him.

"Sorry. My mistake. You *girls*," he said, moving to the phone.

Gladys stopped him with a hand on his arm, beseeching him silently as she said, "I know it's what we *should* do but no one says we have to do it this very second. Let's wait to make that call. Maybe Jason will be back tomorrow and everything will work itself out on its own. No sense in dragging in outsiders if we don't have to."

"You sure?" he asked, torn between wanting to make that call and wanting to reassure Gladys that everything was going to be fine. She nodded and his shoulders tensed even though he let out a gusty sigh. He turned to the girls. "Looks like you're going to bunk here tonight until we get things figured out. Alexis, I need you to help your sisters get settled in. The little one looks about ready to fall over, she's so tired. You been driving all night with your daddy?"

"Yeah."

"I thought so. Your great-aunt Gladys is real tired. She's not feeling good right now. What say we look at this problem with fresh eyes in the morning?"

"I guess." Her arm went around the baby protectively. "Where are we gonna sleep?" she asked after giving the entire room a quick once-over as if assessing the space herself. "That couch over there is big enough, I s'pose."

"There's no need for you girls to curl up on the couch. You can sleep in the guest bedroom. There's a bed big enough for the three of you. All right?"

"I seepy, Lexie." The little one's mouth stretched in a yawn so big it nearly knocked her over, then an awful, wet-sounding cough followed that John had a feeling needed antibiotics to clear up.

"She sick?" He gestured at the little one and Alexis picked up her baby sister as if to shield her, although as thin as all the girls were it just made the whole scene more pathetic and worrisome. "That cough doesn't sound good."

"It's just a cough. She'll be fine," Alexis said, but there was something in those blue eyes that told him she was more worried than she wanted to let on and it made him wonder how long that baby girl had been making those wet, gurgling sounds in her chest. His gut reaction told him she needed a doctor. And he was rarely wrong when his instincts started to clang like cowbells. But he didn't think it warranted a trip to the emergency so there wasn't much he could do about it until morning. He shot Gladys a meaningful look and she gave an imperceptible nod telling him she knew where his thoughts were going and agreed.

"Time to hit the hay," he said.

Gladys smiled her gratitude and sank a little farther into his chair as if it were swallowing her up and he shook his head at the circumstances. He'd always had a soft spot for lost critters and rehabilitating abused horses was part of his livelihood, but he never figured his tender side might catch him three lost little girls. "All right, Gladys, you ought to be in bed, too. You can take the other guest bedroom."

"Are you sure?" she asked, but her expression filled with ill-disguised relief. "I don't mean to be making trouble."

He helped her out of the chair. "Who are you kidding, old woman. You're nothing but trouble."

His comment elicited a weak chuckle as she allowed him to walk her down the hall and into the cold bedroom. He got her settled with a few extra blankets and as he turned to leave so she could change and climb into bed, her voice stopped him at the door frame. "Thank you, Johnny. I know this isn't your idea of a fun time. Tomorrow, we'll get out of your hair. I'll figure something out. It's not your problem and I'm sorry for dumping it in your lap. I…panicked a little. I know I shouldn't have but, oh, what a mess."

He nodded but otherwise remained silent. Gladys was the closest thing he had to a mother. If she had a problem, it was his problem, too. "See you in the morning, Gladys," he said and shut the door.

Returning to the living room where the girls remained, color returning to their cheeks as the fire warmed their frozen little bodies, Alexis ventured forward, surprising him with her question.

"Mister…" Alexis said hesitantly. "Before we go to bed do you got anything we could eat? Bread or something?"

"Let me guess…no dinner?"

Alexis gave a short shake of her head but didn't elaborate. A curse danced behind his teeth as he picked up clearly what she hadn't said. Probably missed more than a few meals here and there judging by the sharp points of their shoulders. Neglect was a form of abuse, too. He'd saved more animals from the brink of starvation than he cared to count but seeing the evidence of neglect in children made his stomach clench with disgust. This was why he kept himself apart from nearly everyone except for the handful of family he had. On the whole, most people disappointed and annoyed him. In this case, he went way past annoyed and straight into pissed off.

"Follow me," he instructed, his voice gruffer than he intended and he winced inwardly as he saw the baby flinch, her rail-thin arms clutching at her sister's neck. *Ah hell*…he cursed himself for scaring her. These kids were traumatized to varying degrees but he could see the baby was particularly jumpy. He needed to treat them as he would a traumatized horse. Voice calm yet firm. Trying again, he said, "Let's see what we can rustle up."

He walked to the kitchen and flipped the light as he went. Reaching into the fridge he pulled out the beans and rice that he'd made earlier in the day.

Alexis had set the baby down to come and peer into the pots as he put them on the stove to reheat. "What's this?" she asked, her eyes wary.

"Beans and rice. All I got on such short notice. Take it or leave it."

Chloe scrambled to the table and climbed into the chair despite the fact that it was way too big for her small frame. The thick oak chair nearly swallowed the toddler but she didn't seem to care as she eyed the pots with blatant desire. "I like beans," she said.

Taylor joined her sister. "Me, too."

John looked to Alexis but she was too busy checking out her surroundings. When she took her tentative spot at the table, he surmised that beans and rice were okay with her.

He grabbed three bowls, heaped a mound of rice and then dumped a ladleful of beans on top and handed the girls their dinner.

They shoveled the food into their mouths without reservation and as one bite cleared the spoon, they were digging in for the next. He wanted to ask when they'd eaten last but a part of him didn't want to know. It would just intensify the burn that was already stoking his temper.

He decided to keep them talking in the hopes that the food would distract them into divulging some details about their situation. "So, where you girls from?"

"Arizona," Taylor answered, scooping the last of her beans onto her spoon with her fingers. She looked to him with her empty bowl, her small tongue snaking out to lick her lips. "Is there more?"

Alexis looked up from her bowl. "Don't be a little piglet."

Taylor shot Alexis a scowl. "I'm no piglet. But I'm still hungry."

John smiled and took Taylor's bowl. "There's plenty more where that came from. I made extra this time around."

He handed Taylor her refilled bowl and focused on Alexis who seemed intent on her supper yet John got the sense that she was covertly taking everything in.

"What's your mom's name?" he asked.

Alexis ignored John's question and, noticing that Chloe had stopped eating, pushed her bowl away. "We're tired. Can we go to bed now?"

"Chloe's not finished with her supper," he said.

Alexis squared her jaw but remained silent. He wondered what was going through her head.

Sighing, he decided this battle wasn't worth fighting. He wasn't going to get any answers tonight. He was looking into the face of a child who knew something about keeping secrets. He hated to think of what the kid was hiding from. "All right, no more questions. Bedtime."

The ranch house was plenty big enough for three small, uninvited guests and an elderly companion but the house rarely had so many people milling around, not since he and Evan were kids and their mom had once rented the extra rooms out to help make ends meet.

He gave them each one of his T-shirts to sleep in and after they'd changed in the adjoining bathroom, they ran to the bed.

Alexis helped Chloe up and Taylor climbed up by herself.

"You need anything else?" he asked gruffly.

"Mister—"

"John," he corrected Chloe.

"Mr. John, do you have a mommy here?"

"A mommy?"

Alexis clarified. "She means do you have a wife?"

He shook his head. "No. Just me and the horses."

Taylor, who had already snuggled into the pillows, sat up with a gap-toothed grin. "Horses?"

"That's right. This is a horse ranch. I've got about ten stabled right now. Why? You like horses?"

Taylor nodded. "Can I see them tomorrow?"

He didn't want to make promises. The first order of tomorrow would be to call the authorities. "We'll see."

Clicking off the light, he closed the door but not before catching a glimpse of Alexis's face turned to the window, an incredibly sad expression on her young profile.

He suspected that little girl felt responsible for her sisters but there was only so much a child could do. It wasn't right. But it happens. That was something he knew well. He just hated seeing it because it dredged up a litany of feelings he'd buried a long time ago. Something about that little girl's expression poked and prodded at the tender spot in his heart in the same way an animal did that everyone else would rather give up on than save.

And to be honest, he didn't know how he felt about that but he suspected his quiet life was about to get noisy.

Chloe coughed, the sound worrying him. No matter what else happened tomorrow, at the very least he was taking that baby to the doctor.

RENEE DOLLING DROVE SLOWLY down the dirt driveway, glancing once again at the address she'd scratched on a piece of paper before leaving Arizona, and prayed that Jason's great-aunt hadn't moved in the ten-plus years since she'd last seen the old woman. From what she remembered, Gladys Stemming was a mouthy one although harmless. But then, Renee had only met her once and who knew what she was like now.

She'd come here as a last-ditch effort. She'd been to all the usual places Jason used to frequent in their neck of the woods in Arizona and had come up empty. Far as Renee knew, Gladys was Jason's only living relative so it served to reason, he might've taken the kids there before he split. If they weren't here…

Think positive. You've gotten this far, don't give up now.

She went to the door and knocked, the absolute stillness of the countryside unnerving her. She knocked again, harder than the first time but the sound just echoed into the inky dark. She glanced around, noted the absence of a vehicle as well as any other sign of civilization and fought the wave of despair. She didn't even know if this was where Gladys still lived. *Okay. Focus. Look for some kind of sign that she does,* Renee instructed herself so she didn't dissolve into a puddle of frustrated tears. Walking across the short porch, she peered into a window and saw the lumps of furniture but nothing that might tell her who lived there.

She rubbed her arms briskly. She'd forgotten how cold it got here. Stomping her feet to keep the circulation moving, she caught the shadowed outline of the mailbox at the end of the driveway. Climbing into the car, she drove to the edge of the road and pulled open the mailbox to feel inside.

Bingo.

Pulling a stack of mail, she glanced at the address and nearly went weak with relief. Gladys Stemming. She still lived here. But even as she thumbed through the hefty stack her elation was short-lived. Apparently, it'd been at least a week since the mail was picked up, which could mean the old woman hadn't been home for a while. Replacing the mail, she chewed her bottom lip. She'd have to come back tomorrow, maybe go into town and ask around. Somebody was bound to know where the old woman was and perhaps, if Gladys had them, her children.

Putting the car into drive, she looked down at the bedraggled and ugly stuffed rabbit that had belonged to Taylor. Renee had found it, abandoned, at their old house after she'd gotten out of rehab. That was four months ago. She'd been searching for him and the girls ever since. Renee didn't much care where Jason went—heaven help him if she managed to get her hands around his neck for this latest stunt—but she needed her girls.

Tears pricked her eyes again but she sniffed them back. She was close. She could feel it.

A fresh flood of anger followed. Damn you, Jason. *Where the hell have you taken my kids?*

Renee reluctantly drove away, refusing to believe that her children were far, that Jason had taken them to a place where she'd never find them. She tried to ignore the guilt that rose to slap her in the face whenever she let herself remember that she was the first one to walk out on their children.

It wasn't her proudest moment but hitting rock bottom usually isn't. Admitting to herself she was an alcoholic trapped in a loveless marriage was a tough pill to swallow, and even as she was committed to sobriety the price had been pretty steep.

Ten long years of missteps and mistakes with Jason, a man who had less depth than a cartoon character. It was enough to make her want to hide in shame over every bad decision she and Jason had put their girls through but she'd vowed things would be different once she got out of rehab.

Only to find them gone. Renee imagined Jason made the decision to take off shortly after she told him she wanted a divorce. He'd known this was the best way to hurt her. And damn, he knew her well.

Every day without her girls felt like knives in her heart.

CHAPTER TWO

THE FOLLOWING MORNING just as he always did, John rose at 5:30 a.m. to start the day and for a split second, as he set the coffee to percolating and stoked the coals in the fireplace to a fresh blaze with kindling and a small piece of seasoned oak, he almost forgot that he wasn't alone. But when a person had been a bachelor as long as John there were some things that didn't slip your notice. Such as the prickling feeling at the back of your neck when you know someone is behind you, staring. He turned and found Taylor standing in the archway, scratching her leg with her toe, her eyes fixed on him.

"Go back to bed. It's too early."

"You're up." She pointed out as she scrubbed at her pixie nose with her palm, her gaze wide and expectant.

"I'm a grown-up. You're still a kid—" *practically still in diapers* "—and kids need their rest. Don't you want to grow up big and strong?"

She thought about it for a second before nodding but then said, "But I can't rest if I'm not sleepy. Can *you,* Mr. John?"

Not really. He didn't much see the point in lounging in bed if he wasn't tired, either. But if he didn't send her back to bed with her sisters, he'd have to find something to entertain her with and he didn't have a clue as to how to entertain a five-year-old little girl. He eyed her speculatively. "You hungry?"

She nodded eagerly. "Are we having more of them beans?" she chirped as she followed him into the kitchen. "They were real good. You're a good cooker, Mr. John."

"I don't know about that, and stop calling me Mr. John. Just John, okay?"

"Okay," Taylor agreed easily, plopping into the chair she'd taken last night. "What's for breakfast, then?"

"Oatmeal." He caught her expression falter and he added quickly, "Or eggs. Take your pick."

"Eggs, please. I like them all mixed up. Do you like them that way? Chloe doesn't like eggs so maybe she could have the oatmeal. But me and Lexie like eggs a lot. Chloe didn't like the way Daddy made his eggs, she said they tasted funny. I didn't think so but sometimes he made her a special kind. Maybe she didn't like just his special eggs because when Lexie made eggs she ate 'em right up. Do you make them special, Mr. John?"

The dizzying speed of the child's twisting and nearly nonsensical dialogue almost had John staring in confusion as he tried to decipher even a quarter of what she'd said but something in that monologue had struck a chord of alarm. "Special eggs, Taylor?"

"Yeah, sometimes he made Chloe her own eggs but—" Taylor's little face scrunched in distaste "—they always made her tummy hurt afterward. Maybe Daddy wasn't a very good cooker."

"Maybe not," John murmured, though he was starting to feel a little sick to his stomach himself. "How come your Daddy always made Chloe her own special eggs?"

Taylor shrugged. "I dunno. But Daddy yells at Chloe a lot."

"Why's that?"

"He just does." Taylor's expression dimmed with sadness and John felt something in his chest pull. Her voice dropped to a scared whisper. "She gets lots of spankings."

Chloe was hardly more than a baby. No one should be raising a hand to her little body.

John stiffened at the anger pouring through his veins at what he was hearing and moved to the fridge to grab the eggs. He'd heard enough and by the time he filled the sheriff's ear with what he'd learned, there was no way in hell those kids were going back to that son of a bitch. He offered a smile to the little tyke even though he was itching to put his fist through the wall, and went through the motions of cooking up a batch of mixed-up eggs that weren't *special* in any way.

GLADYS DIDN'T LOOK VERY GOOD, John thought as he brought her a cup of coffee.

"You sure you don't want to go see that doc of yours?" he asked.

She waved away his concern. "I'm fine. Just a little winded is all from the excitement last night. I just don't know what to do about those poor babies. I don't even know if they've been in school or what kind of lives they've been living. I'm just beside myself."

"What about the mother? Do you know where she might be? Maybe I could place a few calls."

Gladys made a look of distaste. "Oh, don't waste your time with that one. I only met her once but she never made much of an impression. A little snooty and stand-offish if you ask me and we never really hit it off. Not that I was close with Jason, mind you, but at least he was family. I've known him since he was a boy. Never had much of a character. Nothing like you and Evan. If you boys had been anything like Jason your mama would've lost the ranch the moment the tax man had started calling. No…I knew from the time he was a young man he wasn't going to amount to much but I'd hoped I was wrong. There's no satisfaction in being right in this instance."

"So you think the mother just took off or something like Jason did?"

Gladys sighed. "I don't know but what kind of mother would leave her babies behind? I can only imagine," she said, her voice catching as the ghost of an old pain reappeared.

John agreed privately but allowed the quiet to dull the edge of Gladys's long-ago loss. Even after all this time Gladys felt the agony of her stillborn son. He supposed that was a hurt that never truly healed. Not even with decades of time as a balm.

"So what do we do?"

Gladys looked at him sharply then sighed. "We? Oh, Johnny, this isn't your problem. I'll figure something out."

"Don't be ridiculous," he said. "You're in no shape to be tending to three little kids. And frankly, I don't care what you say, I think you need to see your doctor. That surgery might've taken more out of you than you realize."

Gladys was silent for a moment and John had a feeling she was wrestling with her pride, which was no small thing. She wasn't accustomed to being dependent on someone else and it was probably killing her. But it was a temporary thing and she realized this, too, and finally nodded in agreement.

"You might be right," she conceded with a sigh. "And I've been thinking about what you said about contacting the authorities. Maybe that's the best thing to do. I don't think Jason or Renee were doing a great job with these girls. Chloe is most definitely going to need an antibiotic for that cough and something tells me she's been sick for a while. The poor baby has no color to speak of. They ought to have to work to get them back. Maybe it'll teach them a lesson in being parents."

"So you're saying you're okay with me calling the sheriff?"

"Yes, on one condition…the children stay together. They need each other."

"I'll make the call," he said, moving to grab the phone. "And then I'm taking Chloe to the doctor."

RENEE PULLED TO A STOP and took a cursory glance around the ranch that bordered Gladys's property. She'd waited two agonizing days, but by 11 a.m. the third day Renee figured she ought to start poking around. If Gladys had gone on vacation, she might've left instructions with a neighbor to watch the house for her. Either way, Renee might get some kind of information that might be useful in finding Jason and the kids.

She was nearly to the door when a deep voice startled her.

"Didn't you see the sign?"

Her heart jackhammering in her chest, she stammered a bit as she turned, her gaze catching the sign he was talking about. Trespassers Will Be Shot. No Exceptions. She swallowed and got straight to the point. "I'm sorry…I'm looking for Gladys Stemming but she doesn't seem to be home and I wondered…"

"What do you want with Gladys?"

She frowned at his tone. "I'm Renee Dolling. Uh, well, she's my aunt, by marriage, and I—" Why was she explaining herself to this man? Renee straightened. "Has she gone on a trip? If so, do you know when she'll be back?"

"Dolling?" He repeated, a sudden shrewd light entering the hard stare coming at her from beneath a dusty and worn baseball cap. Little ducktails of dirty blond hair too long to be fashionable stuck out from under the hat as if to clearly state he had no time for such niceties as regular haircuts. And his sun-darkened face had a boyish charm that was completely at odds with the stern expression pinching his mouth as he said again, "Did you say your name was Dolling?"

"Yes...do I know you?"

"Name's John Murphy and, no, we've never met, but you've sure got some explaining to do."

"Excuse me?"

"Three days ago your husband dumped your kids with a sixty-seven-year-old woman and took off without so much as a 'see you later' and she'd just had surgery for a triple bypass but you wouldn't know that now, would you, because you dumped your kids before he did."

"He's not my husband," she muttered yet felt heat blooming in her cheeks at his words. *At least he wouldn't be in a few months.* The divorce wasn't quite final in the eyes of the courts but as far as she was concerned Jason could take a long walk off a short pier after the hell he'd put her through. *Selfish bastard.* Wait a minute... "Did you just say my husband dropped the girls off with Gladys?"

"I did."

A relieved smile broke through her annoyance at being interrogated and she exhaled loudly. "Oh, thank God. Where is she? I've been looking for the girls for months and I've been worried sick."

Her relief was short-lived as the man continued to openly assess her, as if he were weighing something heavy in his mind, and unease fluttered in her stomach. "Is there a problem?" she asked stiffly.

"I'd say so."

"Which is?"

"You don't have custody any longer."

Renee's knees nearly snapped out from under her as she sucked in a pained gasp. "What?"

"Yesterday afternoon your girls were placed in the protective custody of their aunt Gladys as a temporary measure until things can be sorted out. No mother, no father…Gladys was their closest relative. Simple as that."

"Well, I'm back so that won't be necessary, now will it?"

"Doesn't work that way. Courts are involved. Convince *them* you've decided to be a mom again and then we'll see. But, can't say that will be easy. Seems the courts around here don't take lightly to parents abandoning their kids."

She bristled at the thinly veiled disgust behind his seemingly mild statement and allowed the building anger to hold the panic at bay.

He didn't have the right to judge her. No one did. "Not that it's any of your business but my reasons for leaving my children with *their father* are my own. I didn't know he was going to do what he did. Just point me in the direction of my children and we'll get out of your life."

"I already told you I can't do that." He shifted lazily against the fence he was leaning against, the slow action belying the fierce set of his jaw.

"What?"

"You heard me. The girls are in Gladys's custody. If

you want your kids, you're going to have to talk to the court."

"This is ridiculous," Renee said, her voice hitting a shrill note. "What the hell is going on here? Are you telling me that you're keeping my girls from me? You're *stealing* my children?" Her voice rose to a hysterical pitch on that last question while her heart beat so hard it felt as if it might burst right out of her chest. This wasn't happening. This had to be a bad dream. A horrific, horrible dream. Total strangers didn't just get to keep other people's kids. It just didn't happen.

"No. The way I see it, three little girls were abandoned by their no-account parents and the law stepped in to protect them. If that's not the way you see it, then you need to prove otherwise to the judge. Until then, get off my property."

CHAPTER THREE

JOHN WATCHED AS THE BLONDE marched over to her car. She shot him one last burning look filled with animosity but he didn't care. Something Taylor had said was still sticking in his mind in a terrible way. Was it possible that their father had put something bad into the baby's eggs? And if so, did the mom know about it? He watched as the woman, Renee, climbed into her car and slammed the door. No doubt she was wishing his head were caught between the door and the chassis. She sat in her car glaring at him, clearly debating her next move.

The front door opened and Gladys appeared with the children flocked around her, each bundled in an odd assortment of secondhand clothes that looked old enough to earn a spot in a museum somewhere, and John knew that any chance of a peaceful resolution was over.

"Lexie?" The woman had jumped from the car and was now running toward the girls until John blocked her path with a warning that she didn't heed. "Get out of my way," she said in a low growl. "Those are my girls and you're not going to stop me from at least seeing them!"

John turned to Gladys, who was watching the scene with alarm, and instructed the older woman to go back inside with the kids.

"Those are my kids! You can't keep me from them. I have a right to see them. Let me go or you and I will have major problems that go way beyond your manners and rude disposition. Do you hear me?"

"I hear you just fine. Now you listen to me. I don't know you from Adam but I do know you're not going anywhere near those girls until we get things sorted out. They've been through plenty without you traipsing into their lives acting like you're here to pick up lost luggage after a long plane ride."

She paled and her bottom lip actually trembled slightly but John wasn't swayed. Where had she been when her girls were going without food? When Chloe got sick and had no one to take her to the doctor? Those little girls needed someone to champion them and right now, he was it.

"You don't know anything about my life."

"About that you're right and, woman, I don't care to know. *You* walked out on your kids. Their *daddy* walked out on them. I didn't ask for this but it landed in my lap just the same and I'll be damned if I'm going to let those girls go to the first ditzy broad who comes my way saying she wants her babies back." She gasped and he gave her arm a little shove as he released her. "Now, the best thing you can do right this minute is to get off my property before I have you arrested for trespassing."

Tears welled in her eyes but she didn't let them fall. Rubbing at her arm where he'd kept a firm grip, she sent him a scathing look and promised to return with the authorities.

"You can't just keep someone's kids like you would a stray puppy! They're mine and you can't—"

"Yack, yack, yack. You do what you feel is necessary. Until then, get lost."

RENEE DROVE LIKE A CRAZY WOMAN straight to the Sheriff's Department in Emmett's Mill, part of her sobbing with elation that she'd finally found her girls and the other part railing at the asshole who had the audacity to keep them from her as if he had the right.

Coming to an abrupt stop in front of the police station, she pushed open the double doors and stalked inside. She approached the reception desk and banged on the little bell for service when the woman behind the desk was slow to open the sliding protective glass window.

"I need to talk to an officer right away," she said to the dispatcher-receptionist, ignoring the woman's look of annoyance. "A man is keeping my children from me and I need an officer to go out there and get them."

"Excuse me? Come again? You say someone's holding your kids?"

"Yes. A man named John Murphy—"

"That name sounds awful familiar…does he own the Murphy ranch out on the outskirts of town?"

"Yeah, I guess it was a ranch of some kind." She vaguely remembered seeing a few horses and a dog. Renee let out a short breath as incredulity warred with extreme frustration at the woman's failure to grasp that a serious crime was being committed. She seemed more interested in playing the Name Game, and Renee tried again. "Yeah, it was a ranch but I hardly think that's relevant when I'm trying to tell you that this John Murphy has *kidnapped* my children. He has my kids and I want them right now. Can I speak with a deputy please?"

"Don't get huffy." The woman's mouth pinched, causing little lines to crease her lips in a most unflattering way. "All the available deputies are out on a call. But if you leave a name and number—"

Renee slapped her hand down on the counter, making the woman jump and her hand flutter to her chest in alarm but Renee was past caring about making waves. She wanted her kids. "I will not. A crime is being committed and I want a goddamn officer. Do you hear me?"

The woman's deep-set eyes narrowed and Renee knew she'd just crossed over to the place of No Return and she was pretty sure that place was also nicknamed Up Shit Creek Without a Paddle because moments later, those deputies that were previously unavailable came pouring out and Renee found herself in handcuffs.

"What are you doing?" Renee shrieked as the deputy led her to a small single cell in the rear of the building. "I come here for help and you're arresting me?"

"Nancy pressed the panic button, which means you must've done something to cause her to panic. This is for everyone's safety until we figure out what's going on."

A woman officer entered the room. "I got this Fred. You can go ahead and take that coffee break you were wanting earlier." She waited for Deputy Do-Right Fred to leave and then she introduced herself. "I'm Sheriff Casey. Seems you're making friends wherever you go. I got a call from John Murphy about a half hour before you showed up and started abusing my staff. Want to tell me what's going on?"

Renee's cheeks warmed at the cloaked rebuke and took a minute to calm herself before she answered. "My ex-husband, Jason Dolling, took off with our kids and I've been trying to find them for the past four months. I remembered that Jason had a great-aunt in the area and so I came looking for my girls here and found them at the neighbor's house!"

"Are you sure they're your kids?"

Renee stared at the woman. "Are you kidding me? Of course I know for sure. They're *my* kids. That's not something you forget."

"According to John, you walked out on them. That true?"

"I left them with their father for personal reasons," Renee said, fuming. "I don't see how that's relevant."

"I'm the one asking the questions. Why'd you leave them?"

"I told you. It was personal."

"Yeah…it usually is." The woman regarded her shrewdly and Renee felt her jaw tense. She got the distinct impression this small-town sheriff was judging her and there was nothing Renee hated more than to be put on display just so someone else could offer their opinion. The sheriff sighed. "Well, we've got ourselves a situation."

"Yes, I agree. Some hillbilly horse rancher has my children and I require your assistance to retrieve them," Renee said.

"That's not exactly how I see it," the sheriff admitted with a shake of her head.

"Oh? Is there any other way to see things? Perhaps you'd like to swab my cheek for DNA to make sure I'm their mother."

The sarcasm in her voice did little to soften the sheriff toward her but Renee was losing patience with this whole ridiculous routine. And to think she'd thought the hardest part of this mess would've been to find Jason and the girls, not pick them up. Noting the narrowed stare and gathering frown on the sheriff's face, she tried again. "Listen, I'm tired and I just want to get my girls. It seems there's been a misunderstanding but no harm done. So if you'll just provide a police escort, we'll be out of your hair before you know it and everything can go back to the way things were before me and my girls ever stepped foot in this godfor—" she checked that part of her sentence "—uh, town."

The sheriff smiled but Renee felt the chill before the woman started talking. "You never answered my question." At Renee's blank stare, the sheriff asked again, "Why'd you leave your kids behind with a man who, by the sounds of it, wasn't fit to water a dog much less care for three babies?"

No one hated the truth of that answer more than her, but if she lied it would only make her look worse so Renee grit her teeth and admitted her greatest shame to a total stranger. "Because I was in rehab."

"Rehab."

In that one word, Renee heard a wealth of condemnation and she wanted to scream. She'd get no help from the sheriff. Fine. *On to Plan B.* Inside she was shaking with frustration but she kept her expression calm, knowing if she had any chance of getting her girls she had to first get the hell out of this jail cell.

The sheriff sighed. "Okay, here's the deal. John told me Gladys Stemming has temporary guardianship for the time being so until you get in front of the judge and have that amended, the order stands and I can't let you charge out there and take the kids. But seeing as you haven't actually committed a crime I can't keep you here so, if I let you out of this cell, you're going to promise me that you're not going to rattle any more cages with your screeching and hollering. That's not how things are done around here, you hearing me?"

Renee swallowed and nodded though it killed her

to agree to those terms, especially when her first instinct was to drive straight back to that ranch and take the girls and run. Fortunately, good sense prevailed and she rationalized that once she got in court—in front of someone normal instead of these small-town hillbilly types who made up the rules as they went along—she knew she'd get her girls back and they could leave this nightmare behind.

"I hear you. Loud and clear," Renee answered. "I'm sorry for freaking out your receptionist. I was upset. I haven't seen my girls in months and contrary to what you may think about me, I've been desperately searching for them since Jason took off," she added, with a dose of humility that wasn't entirely fake for she really hadn't meant to frighten anyone.

"Um-hmm. Well, just see that you keep your nose clean until you can get to court. I don't want to have to lock you up again."

That makes two of us.

JOHN SAT ACROSS THE TABLE from Alexis and Taylor while Chloe helped Gladys bake cookies in the kitchen.

"Was that your mama?" he asked the girls. Both were wearing solemn expressions, though there was a hint of anger in Alexis's. He sighed. "If that woman was your mama, she's going to come back and if the courts decide she's fit, you're going to have to go with her. Don't you want to see your mama?"

Taylor looked uncertain but as she slanted a quick

glance at her older sister, who had remained stoic, she chose to keep her answer locked up tight. Though her silence didn't last long.

"I want to stay with you, Mr. John," Taylor blurted. "I like it here. It's warm and you're a good cooker and I don't mind sharing a bed with my sisters because it's soft and I don't get woken up by bugs running across my toes. Please don't make us leave, Mr. John."

That last part—delivered with a child's earnestness—hit him square in the chest. He didn't want to give the kid false promises but he couldn't imagine breaking her heart like everyone else in her short life had done. "There are rules when it comes to kids," he started, hating that it wasn't as simple as Taylor saw it. "If your mama isn't fit then you have to go to a court appointed something-or-another. This is a temporary thing that we got going on right now." Tears sprang to Taylor's eyes and Alexis pulled her closer. Ah hell… rules were meant to be broken, weren't they? "Listen, I'll see what I can do but if you stay here, there are rules here, too. Chores, helping out. I run a working horse ranch and I don't have time to be chasing after three little girls who aren't prone to listening." He gave Alexis a short look. "Am I clear?"

Taylor nodded. "Can I help with the horses?"

John exhaled loudly, feeling as if he'd just agreed to take on the world for three little strangers. "We'll see. In the meantime, why don't you go help Mrs. Stemming with those cookies. I need to talk with your sister."

He watched as Taylor hopped from her chair and skipped to help Gladys, a bright smile wreathing her small face as Gladys handed her a bowl with cookie dough and told her to start rolling it into little balls for the oven. He'd told Gladys she shouldn't be up and about so much but the old gal wanted to feel useful and wouldn't be deterred. He figured for now it was all right but he was going to get her to see the doctor soon.

Once Taylor was suitably occupied he gestured for Alexis to follow him into the living room, which was a far enough distance from the kitchen to allow them some privacy.

She took a seat opposite him, perched on the edge of the cowhide sofa as if poised to bolt if the need arose. Everything about Alexis, from her rigid posture to her sharp, alert and wary gaze, told him that this girl had lost her childhood somewhere along the way of her life. He could relate somewhat. He'd often felt like Evan's father rather than just his older brother after their mom died. The weight of that responsibility had a tendency to suck the fun right out of growing up. He eyed her intently. This kid didn't know what it was like to be coddled and so he'd talk to her straight.

"You mad at your mama? It's okay if you are. She did a bad thing, leaving you like she did. But it seems maybe she has changed a bit since you saw her last. She seemed real upset, don't you think? Maybe you could sit down and chat with her for a bit, get a feel for what she's saying."

Alexis softened imperceptibly. "What do you mean?"

"Well, I know you still have feelings for your mama and that's okay, too. We can be mad at the people we love. But if you don't talk with her about your feelings, they'll just fester up inside of you and make you sick. It's like having an invisible infection inside your heart and it never gets better unless you treat it."

Alexis gave a stiff nod but remained quiet.

"I need to ask you something about Chloe." At the mention of her baby sister, her demeanor became protective. Her little fists curled and he doubted she even realized it.

"What about Chloe?"

"Was your daddy mean to her?"

"Daddy was mean to all of us."

"Yeah, I get that. He sure as hell ain't up for Father of the Year but I mean did he pick on Chloe more than the rest of you?" At first Alexis seemed reluctant to answer, her small mouth compressed as if trying to hold back what wanted to fall out, so he waited. His patience was rewarded when Alexis started talking in a barely audible whisper.

"Yes," she said, tears glittering in her eyes. "It got really bad when our mom left."

"Do you know why?" he asked gently and Alexis shook her head. Drawing a deep breath, he asked the question that had been bothering him the most. "Do you think your daddy was trying to make Chloe sick?"

Alexis bit the side of her cheek and her face paled as she struggled to hold back the tears that welled in her eyes.

"It's okay, you can tell me. I know you did your best to keep your sisters safe. Tell me what your daddy was doing to Chloe."

Alexis gulped and when she spoke again her voice shook. "Special eggs. He made her eat eggs that he made special and they always made her sick. The last time, right before we left Arizona, I watched him as he made Chloe's breakfast. He put something in it from under the kitchen sink and I know that's not where we keep the salt and pepper. We only keep cleaning supplies down there. So I didn't let her eat them."

"How'd you do that?"

"When he wasn't looking I switched our plates. I knew he hadn't put anything in me and Taylor's eggs and then I told him I didn't feel good. I threw my eggs away. He didn't care about me, but he made sure Chloe ate every bit on her plate before he'd let her get down from the table. I think my daddy—" She stopped on a painful sob and John felt her struggle as if it were his own. Alexis had confirmed his worst fear. The girls' father had been trying to poison his youngest daughter.

He caught Alexis's red-rimmed stare and made her a solemn promise. "You're never going back to that man. And if your mom isn't up to snuff…you aren't going back to her, either. That okay with you?"

Her answer was slow in coming but he suspected it came straight from her heart as she nodded and said, "Fine by me."

Good. First things first… "I'm friends with Sheriff Casey. You need to tell her everything you just told me."

"Are you sure we're not going to go back to Daddy?" she asked, her eyes scared.

"Not if I have anything to say about it."

"Daddy was real mean to Chloe," she said. "I'm afraid of what he'll do if we go back. He told Chloe if she didn't stop peeing her panties he'd put her outside like a dog because she smelled like one. He left her out there for hours in the rain. I went out and got her after he went to bed. It took all night to warm her up but the cough she has now…it's from that night. Sometimes she coughs so hard, she can't breathe."

"I know, honey, that's why I took her to the doc. She's got some medicine and we're taking care of that nasty cough so you don't need to worry anymore," he said, careful to keep his voice neutral and calm when inside he was to the boiling point. He couldn't imagine little Chloe locked outside, shivering in the rain, crying for her sisters and huddled against the door while her father sat in relative comfort inside the house. God help him if John got his hands on that man. But for now, he needed to lift the weight from this little girl's shoulders. "All right. Here's the deal. Sheriff Casey is a good person. There's no way you're going back to your daddy after you tell her what you told me. But you have to be honest with her so she can help. Okay?"

Alexis nodded and wiped at the remaining tears glistening on her downy cheek. "Why did she leave us with him?" she asked quietly, more to herself than to John. Suddenly, she looked at him as if expecting an answer though he didn't have one. "Maybe if she'd taken us with her…Chloe wouldn't have been hurt." She rose and glanced away, seeming much older than she really was. When she spoke again, her voice was cold. "I hate her. No one can make me love her again. Not you. Not anybody. I'll hate her forever and it doesn't matter if she's changed."

As John watched her stalk from the room to join her sisters, he didn't doubt a single emotion flowing from that little girl's strong heart. In a way he felt bad for the storm that was heading in the direction of Renee Dolling. That woman would have to dig deep to find the loving daughter she'd left behind. And, given what the girls had been through, Renee might find her way to China much easier than the way to her daughter's closed-off heart.

He didn't envy her. Not one bit.

CHAPTER FOUR

"COURT RULING STANDS. Temporary guardianship will remain with Gladys Stemming until family court has had a chance to review the case further." The rap of the gavel brought Renee out of her stunned stupor. What had just happened?

She shot from her seat. "Excuse me? What the hell just happened?"

The Honorable Judge Lawrence Prescott II gave her a sharp look just as the bailiff started to move forward to deter her from approaching the bench. "You'll watch your language in my courtroom, miss," he said with a soft drawl that betrayed southern roots somewhere in his lineage. He gestured for her to take her seat and once she reluctantly returned to her chair, he said to his court reporter, who in Renee's opinion looked a lot like the receptionist at the sheriff's department, "Please repeat the judgment for Mrs. Dolling, Nancy."

Renee stared, unable to believe what she was witnessing, as indeed dour-faced sheriff's receptionist Nancy pulled the tape from the machine and repeated in a clipped voice the judgment that had just been rendered.

Schooling her voice into something less screeching and more reasonable, she tried a different tactic. "I heard the judgment. What I don't understand is how the court can appoint a virtual stranger as guardian for my children when I am their mother. They should be with me. Surely, you can understand that?"

Judge Prescott gave her a wintry glare and Renee felt her hopes of putting this nightmare behind her anytime soon freezing to the point of death. "What I understand is that you're a fickle woman prone to bad decisions when it comes to your children. That's what I know about *you*. What I know about Gladys Stemming is that she's solid and dependable." The judge glanced at John Murphy sitting opposite to Renee. "And since Mr. Murphy has offered the use of the ranch while she recuperates from her surgery, it is the court's determination that the children have a safe and stable environment while this whole situation is sorted out. In addition to that, the children themselves have expressed a desire to stay with their aunt…not you."

Renee sucked in a sharp breath at the rejection and blinked back tears. "Sir, if you gave me a chance to talk with my girls I would explain the circumstances and I'd get them to understand. In time, they might even forgive me for making a terrible mistake but if you keep them from me how can I hope to make everything right again? I love my girls and if I had the chance to do things over, I'd do it all much differently."

"Be that as it may, you didn't do things differently and your children suffered. Particularly your youngest."

What did he mean by that? Renee frowned. "Chloe? I don't understand how she suffered the most…"

Judge Prescott peered over his glasses at Sheriff Casey and continued, "Your youngest daughter is suffering from bronchial pneumonia due to horrific abuse at the hands of your ex-husband. The doctor she was taken to discovered old bruises and a hairline fracture in her left arm that had been left to heal on its own."

Renee felt sick. "I wasn't aware…"

"Yes, well, the court isn't interested in your excuses, Mrs. Dolling. The fact remains that you left your children in the hands of a dangerous and abusive man. It is the court's belief that only through the vigilant actions of your other children that Chloe is still alive."

Renee caught the stare of John Murphy—the man who was essentially getting her children—and she expected to see the same condemnation she was getting from the rest of the room, but she saw a flicker of something close to sympathy that took her by surprise. She looked away abruptly. She didn't want his pity—or anyone else's. Not that it was coming her way in waves at the moment but the scraps of her pride demanded she hold her head high. "How long is this temporary arrangement in effect?" she asked.

"As long as I deem necessary."

She took a risk as she said, "Forgive me, Your Honor, but I think it would be more appropriate for my children to go to a state-approved foster home rather than that of some man you happen to know from school. How do I know that this John Murphy isn't some kind of pervert?"

Nancy the court reporter-sheriff's receptionist gasped and her eyes widened before she returned her attention to her typing. Yep. Nancy's reaction pretty much clinched Renee's sinking suspicion she just made things worse, but Renee wasn't going down without a fight.

"I've had just about enough of your mouth," the judge warned. Renee caught Sheriff Casey shaking her head as if Renee was just about the dumbest person on the planet to question the judge in such a manner, but Renee felt desperation setting in and, well, desperate people do dumb things. The judge shuffled his papers from the case and handed them to the court secretary for filing. "Get a job. Get a place to stay and then, when you get your ducks in a row, we'll talk about modification. In spite of your infernal mouth, I get the sense that you didn't know what a monster you'd left your kids with but that doesn't erase what happened to those girls. They need stability. They need someone they can trust. And they trust John and Gladys. I could order them into foster care but that would likely traumatize them more as I'd have to break them up because the system's full. They'd probably even go to separate counties. You want that?"

She couldn't imagine separating the girls. "No," she answered in a small voice.

"Then stop your complaining about how unfair things are *for you* and start focusing on getting your life back together so that your girls would rather be with you than a stranger."

That hurt. Renee swallowed the sharp retort that flew to mind as her defenses went up, because she knew as whacked out and nuts as this whole court drama was, there was a certain kindness directed at her children. If the girls wanted to be with John Murphy for the time being, she'd go along with it. But as soon as she won their trust back, they were packing it out of this place—fast.

GLADYS MET JOHN AT THE DOOR, her expression anxious. He allayed her fears quickly. "Court ruling stands but their mother, Renee, gets monitored visitation for the time being."

"Oh, thank goodness. Those poor babies have been tied up in knots since you left this morning. Alexis takes it the hardest. That poor lamb. I can only imagine what she's been through trying to protect her sisters from that man. It boggles my mind why their mother left those babies in Jason's care."

"In court she mentioned something about being in rehab when Jason split," John said, chewing the side of his cheek as he mulled over the information himself. What kind of rehab she didn't elaborate but drugs of any sort were bad news by his estimation. "But Judge Prescott didn't seem to care much for her excuse. I don't think he much cared for her, not that she helped matters at all. Her mouth sure does overload her ass a lot."

Gladys nodded. "I'm sure. I remember she had quite the smart mouth when I met her all those years ago. I'm just glad Larry was sitting on the bench today instead of a temporary judge that they sometimes bring in from the city to help with the backlog. Someone else less conservative might've given those babies back," she said with a shudder. "Makes me sick to think of it."

He agreed. Judge Prescott was an old-school kind of guy. If the law still allowed a hanging tree, he'd be the kind to supply the rope. "Where are the girls?" he asked, looking around.

She gestured toward the living room, where the faint sound of the television could be heard. He frowned. "I don't think they should be watching so much TV. Rots your brain from what I hear."

Gladys shooed him. "Stop being such a bear. Those babies could use a little pampering. Besides, now that we've gotten the court stuff out of the way we can start getting the older girls enrolled in school. They're going to need some routine and stability after what they've been through and school will keep their minds busy. I've already placed a few calls. It's going to be a couple days before we can track down Alexis's transcripts but until then they're going to need some clothes. They can't go to school in those rags."

He'd already been thinking about that, seeing as the clothes they showed up in weren't fit to line a dog's bed. "Maybe I could pick up a few pairs of jeans at the hardware store," he speculated, which earned him a scowl from Gladys.

"Hardware store? You can't put Rustlers on a bunch of girls. What's wrong with you? They need pretty things, not work boots and coveralls. Leave it to me. I'm handy on the computer and Macy's delivers anywhere in the United States."

John fished his wallet out from his back pocket and pulled his credit card free from the plastic holder. He handed it to Gladys. "Buy them whatever they need," he said. "I don't care how much it costs."

"John…that's too generous," Gladys protested softly but her eyes shone with love. She tucked the card into her apron pocket and gave his cheek a pat. "You're a good man, Johnny. Now, go on and do something useful. Don't you have horses to tend to?"

He did and Gladys giving him the go-ahead should've been a relief but he felt oddly compelled to check on the girls himself. He supposed that was only natural given the extreme circumstances but it still knocked him silly at odd moments that he was even in this situation. Him. The bachelor. With a house full of kids that he barely knew.

And despite his stern instruction not to, his thoughts kept pulling him in the direction of Renee. She ought to be the last person he was thinking about—just the fact that he was gave him serious pause—but he'd be a liar if he didn't admit where his thoughts kept wandering. She truly looked stricken when the judge told her of Chloe's injuries. Either she was a really good actress or she felt sick inside at the knowledge that her ex-husband had abused her baby. But the question that nagged at John was, why only Chloe? It seemed Jason Dolling had singled out that poor kid—not that he was going to win any parenting awards—but the other girls seemed to have been spared the brunt of his anger. Little Chloe didn't fare the same. A shudder of discomfort shook him as he realized just how close Chloe may have come to leaving this world if it hadn't been for her sisters, mostly Alexis, looking out for her. The doc found traces of arsenic lingering in Chloe's system from the repeated doses slipped into her "special eggs." Doc said she should be fine now but a few more doses and it could've been fatal. Peeking around the corner, he spied the three towheaded girls snuggled up to one another, watching television, and he knew there would be hell to pay if anyone—including their dingbat mother—tried to hurt them again.

He didn't understand his own vehemence but he knew enough not to question it. What was true, was true and the protective feelings curling around his heart were solid even if he didn't understand where they were coming from.

A FEW DAYS LATER, RENEE returned to the ranch that was her children's temporary home and realized her palms were sweating. She could still see Alexis's frozen expression, caught between her previous happiness and shock, and knew she was the cause of her daughter's unpleasant reaction.

She knew better than to expect her daughters to run to her with open arms—least of all Alexis—but the open rejection hurt a lot more than she imagined it would. Today was the first of their scheduled visitations and Renee was going to make the most of her time with her girls. She didn't chase them all over California and back again to give up now. She'd help them to understand why she left and why she would never leave them again. Renee fingered the small badge pinned in a discreet corner on the lapel of her jacket and prayed for strength before exiting the car and walking toward the house.

But before she reached the front door, that infernal rancher, John, once again intercepted her and she wanted to throw something heavy his way. She didn't even try to hide her scowl as she said, "It's my court appointed visitation day. Check your paperwork."

"I know what day it is. I just want a few words first."

She tensed. "Why?"

"I want to make sure you don't try to pressure the girls into doing something they don't want to do."

"Excuse me?"

"I know you don't think much of this arrangement. It's pretty much written all over your face, much the same as it was in the courtroom, that you think this is a bunch of bullshit but at this point you're in no place to judge. I don't care about you or your feelings. All I care about is that those little girls aren't hurt again by either of their parents. And let me give you a fair warning right now…if that ex-husband of yours even comes near these kids, I won't hesitate to shoot him just for the sheer fun of it. So, if you and him are still cozy, make sure you give him that message. I'm not one to kid about things this important. You hearing me, Mrs. Dolling?"

Her first instinct was to slap him across his scruffy face for the insult he so casually tossed her way. Hadn't he heard her when she said Jason *stole* their kids and she'd been chasing after them ever since? The very thought of being friendly much less *cozy* with Jason made her physically ill. But the very fact that this man who was no blood relation to her children was championing them in a way that their own father had not kept her hot words and temper in check—though the action was not without great effort on her part.

"I hear you just fine. I'm not deaf," she said, meeting his steady gaze without flinching. She imagined that when this man stared people down he won most of the time. He was the kind of man who gave no quarter but expected none, either, yet somehow her girls had found the one soft spot in his heart and he wasn't letting go. Her stomach gave a discomforting tingle and she slammed the door shut on wherever her thoughts were going. "Are you finished? I've waited months to see my kids. Despite your scintillating conversation skills, I didn't come to see you."

"Fair enough. I just wanted to make sure we're clear. They're inside. Mrs. Stemming will monitor your visit. Don't give her any grief, either. She's taken to the girls and I won't have you upsetting her."

What a wonderful opinion he had of her. "As long as she doesn't give me any grief, I won't feel the need to dish it out."

And with that she started walking straight up the steps to the house. She didn't wait for his approval or his invitation and gave the front door a solid knock. Her bravado did wonders for the appearance that she wasn't scared to death of her own children but did little to stop her hands from shaking or her knees from weakening. She glanced over her shoulder and saw John watching her intently, his eyes never leaving her. She suppressed a shudder at that strong stare and knocked again. This time, the door opened and an older woman with a full head of white hair stood between her and her girls.

Renee tried putting on a cheerful face. No sense in making enemies purposefully, her own aunt used to say. "Hello…Aunt Gladys," she said, trying for some sense of familiarity, hoping that it might soften any lingering hard feelings. "It's been a long time. I'm Renee."

"I know who you are." Gladys's expression was pinched and disapproving as she moved aside. "Come in. They're waiting for you."

Mean old bat. Wiping her slick palms across the seat of her pants she followed the older woman into the expansive ranch house and despite the foreign surroundings could sense that this house was warm and inviting with its lived-in look and strong masculine accents. She rounded the corner and there sat her girls, their little faces pulled into solemn masks filled with anxiety and trepidation, and her heart broke from a heavy combination of joy and deep agony.

Chloe sat on Alexis's lap while Taylor sat beside her older sister. The three couldn't have looked more miserable yet stuck to each other as if glued.

Coming forward, wanting desperately to wrap them all in her arms and never let go, she stopped short when she saw Alexis tighten her arms around Chloe protectively. Pain arced through Renee but she didn't want to push the girls too fast. Taking Alexis's lead, she moved to the chair closest to them and took a seat.

"How about some cookies and tea?" Mrs. Stemming broke in with a modicum of manners though there was no warmth directed at Renee in those bright, alert eyes. Renee was tempted to tell her to stick her cookies where the sun didn't shine but she held her tongue in the interest of playing nice. When Gladys spoke again, Renee was glad she'd remained quiet. "Taylor and I made a fresh batch of gingersnaps this morning and they're mighty good," she said, sending a genuine smile to Taylor who returned it tentatively.

Although mildly allergic to ginger Renee smiled and nodded. If suffering through hives was the price she had to pay to win her daughters' love back, she'd eat an entire batch of gingersnaps and risk anaphylactic shock for the privilege. "I'd love some."

But Alexis wasn't going to let her off that easy.

"She hates gingersnaps," Alexis said, her mouth forming a hard line.

"I don't hate them, Lexie," Renee gently corrected. "I'm slightly allergic but I'd love to try Taylor's cookies."

"Whatever."

Renee drew back at the flippant sarcasm in Alexis's voice and her hopes for a happy reunion sank to the bottom of her heart. Gladys looked to Renee for direction and she gave her a weak smile. "I'd still love to try the cookies."

"Are you sure?" Gladys asked, uncertainty etched into her expression, no doubt from the fear that Renee might fall over dead from a simple cookie.

"It'll be fine," Renee assured her. "Promise."

Gladys left the room and Renee sought a safe subject to fill the empty air. "Tell me what you've been doing lately. I want to hear all about your adventures. I've missed out on so much. I have a lot to catch up on. Taylor, sweetheart, why don't you start?"

But before Taylor could open her mouth, Alexis started talking. The anger in her young voice fairly vibrated her body as she spoke.

"What do you wanna know?"

Renee faltered, not quite sure how to talk to this angry stranger. "Anything, honey. I want to hear about everything," she said, her gaze darting to Taylor, hoping for some help from her little chatterbox, but she received none. Taylor remained quiet and wide-eyed, waiting for a cue from her sister on how to act. "Taylor?" she prompted but Alexis shut her down before she could say a word.

"You really wanna know or are you just trying to play like you care?" Alexis said, her gaze hot.

Renee drew back, stung. "Of course I want to know. And I *do* care."

Alexis smirked, the expression on her young face entirely too mature for her actual age of nine and a half. "Okay. Daddy's been trying to kill Chloe by giving her rat poison. He put her outside in the rain when she peed the bed and he used to hit her with his belt until he broke her bones. Do you wanna see the bruises?" Renee could only stare in shock. Alexis shrugged. "You asked. Oh, and I'm a year behind in school because Daddy moved us around too much. And Taylor gets nightmares. Are we done catching up?"

Without waiting for Renee's answer—not that she could've mustered one—Alexis rose with Chloe still in her arms and stalked from the room, calling for Taylor to follow. Alexis whirled before exiting, her blue eyes blazing. "And stop calling me Lexie. I *hate* that name and I never want to hear it again."

Tears sprang to Renee's eyes and she didn't care that the old bat was watching as she let her head sink into her hands. She was a fool to think that Lexie— no, Alexis—would ever forgive her. And rightly so. Who was she to even ask for forgiveness when her children had suffered so much?

"She's a smart girl," she heard the old woman say,

then crunch into a cookie, presumably the gingersnaps she'd offered earlier. "She's not one to eat up bullshit, if you know what I mean."

She did. Lifting her head, she eyed the woman. "You're no expert on my daughter after spending a few days with her. I'd appreciate if you kept your opinions to yourself," Renee said, standing stiffly.

Gladys shrugged. "Doesn't seem like you're much of an expert, either, and you've been around her for at least some of those nine years she's been on this planet, so I'd watch where you're slinging that attitude of yours," Gladys said before finishing the rest of her cookie.

"I know my daughter," Renee retorted, her cheeks heating but her heart ached privately. What Alexis said… Renee would never have guessed that Jason would have been capable of hurting Chloe. Never even imagined, though she should've figured with his more recent drug history. He'd become unpredictable. She struggled to keep her voice calm. "She's smart. She'll come around."

"Maybe." The older woman nodded, then bit into another cookie. "If she thinks you deserve a second chance."

"She will. I'm her mother."

"Don't get your dander up. I'm just saying she's a smart girl and if you don't blow it by cutting out on them again, she'll likely loosen up. Kids are more forgiving than adults."

"Thanks." The word was difficult against her lips

but she sensed this woman was not her enemy even if she wasn't her friend. She blew out a breath and rolled her shoulders to release the tension building behind her blades. "How are they doing?"

"Good as to be expected I guess. You might want to talk with John, though. He's got all the details you're probably looking for. I just bake and keep them occupied when John has to tend to the horses."

Renee smiled softly, thinking of how Taylor must love being around the horses. "Does Taylor get to see the horses?"

"Oh, yes, that one is hard to keep out of the stables. John lets her help him feed them in the morning, though I suspect when he gets them enrolled in school, she's going to put up a fuss when she can't hang around the barn all day."

Alarm spiked through Renee. "School? He's enrolling them in school? Here?"

Gladys looked nonplussed. "Well, of course, here. Where else? They have to go to school. It's the law. It's bad enough that riffraff of a father dragged them from one place to another with no thought as to how they'd get an education, but the judge was adamant that they get enrolled right away. The only reason they're not enrolled yet is because of some hiccup with Alexis's transcripts."

She supposed that made sense but enrolling them in school suggested permanence and she didn't want the girls to think they were staying any longer than the court order required. And the fact that the judge wanted them enrolled didn't bode well for a quick resolution in Renee's estimation. "Where is the school here?"

"Well, the high school kids get bused to Emmett's Mill or Coldwater but there's an elementary school just down the road a bit that the local country kids go to. That's where they'll go."

"Is it a good school?"

Gladys smiled proudly. "One of the best. It's not big on fancy things like new computers but the teachers are warmhearted and the classes are small. The girls will fit in right away. Don't you worry."

"My girls are strong. They'd fit in anywhere," she bluffed, only hoping that was true. The truth was, as Gladys had already pointed out, she didn't know her girls at all.

But, as her gaze drifted out the front window to the arena where John was working with a horse, she aimed to rectify that no matter what—or who—stood in her way.

CHAPTER FIVE

JOHN CROSSED HIS ARMS across his chest and stared. "You want me to what?"

Renee lifted her chin. "Hire me."

"For what and why?"

"Well, you need someone to help with the girls and by the looks of your house, someone to help out with general upkeep. I figure the best way to stay close to my girls and get to know them again is to be around them as much as possible and I can't do that if I live and work twenty miles away. Plus, there's really not much to choose from as far as jobs go. You live in the sticks of the sticks." Renee paused to take a breath and he realized more was coming. "And, I was thinking that perhaps you could let me stay here in that guest-house you have behind the main house. I'd be out of your way and it would take care of two of the require-ments the judge set forth in the judgment."

"Why would I want you moving into my house? Have you forgotten I don't much like you? And just what the hell are you insinuating about my house?" Was she saying he was a slob? He shot her a dirty look.

"You sure have a funny way of asking for a favor, you know that?"

She returned his glare but the way she chewed her bottom lip told him she realized she might've been a little harsh. "I didn't mean to insult you. All I'm saying is your house is clean enough for a bachelor but a woman's touch is needed around here." She gestured to the drapes at the front window. "When was the last time those things were aired out? Or how about the floor? This old hardwood needs to be waxed every now and again. I figure you don't have the time to be doing stuff like that."

He glanced at the floor. Looked fine to him. So it didn't shine like it used to when his mama was alive but it was still in good shape. And whoever heard of airing out drapes? How dirty could they be? They just hang there. "How do you know so much about cleaning house?" he asked.

She bristled at his open speculation but answered even though he suspected she would've rather told him to shove it and mind his own business. "My mother was a bit of a stickler when it came to keeping a clean home. She was known to fire the staff for not adhering to her standard," she muttered.

Staff? His ears pricked at the small tidbit of information but his interest didn't compel him to inquire further. The woman was becoming a bit of a mystery that only gave him a headache when he tried to figure her out.

He read nothing but honesty as she said, "I just want

to do what's best for the girls, and contrary to what you or that nutty judge may think my girls need their mother."

He could argue they needed their mother to protect them when their father was being a monster but he figured there was no sense in poking at a beehive when you knew full well nothing but pissed off bees were going to fly out. But that didn't mean he wanted her moving in. "I don't want you moving in and I don't need your services," he maintained stubbornly.

She squared her jaw, not willing to give up. "Gladys seems nice enough but you can't really expect an old lady to keep up with three little girls. She can't even lift Chloe and that's who she'd be around when the older girls are in school. What if there was an emergency and you weren't around? Gladys tells me that you work outside a lot. What if she had a heart attack or something?"

"Gladys is fine," he growled. But he knew he couldn't expect Gladys to keep up with the girls and he did worry when he had to be outside for any length of time, which given his trade was hard to get around. Still, having Renee here…at the ranch? It smacked of trouble. "The court might not approve of you being around the girls without supervision."

"I'm not a danger to my own children," she said quietly and John couldn't help but soften a bit toward her. "I just want to get to know them again. This is the easiest and most helpful way for both of us. I need a job and a place to stay. You and Gladys need help with the girls. It's a win-win for us both. And, once the girls and I patch up our relationship, we can all get out of your hair. That's what you want, right?"

"I want what's in the girls' best interests and I don't know if that includes letting them leave with you anytime soon," he snapped, knowing full well he hated the idea of letting the girls leave with this nut but as much as she taxed his patience, she'd made valid points in her favor. "Let me think about it," he said with no small amount of ire in his tone. "I have to talk with the girls first. I don't want to upset them more than I have to. Their first day of school is tomorrow and neither of the older kids is too happy about it."

"Alexis used to love school," Renee murmured, her expression sad. She looked up hopefully. "Maybe I could go with you when you take them."

He slanted his gaze at her, her blue eyes so much like her oldest daughter's that he suspected when Alexis grew up she'd be the spitting image of her mama. If that were the case he'd have to beat the boys off with a stick—that is if the girls were still around here by that time, which wasn't likely. Shifting in annoyance at his thoughts, he grunted an answer.

She blinked at him. "What? I'm sorry…was that a yes or a no?"

"I said fine. Do what you want. Just don't upset the girls."

"What time?"

"I'm supposed to have the girls at the school at

seven-thirty." He chewed the inside of his cheek, wondering if he was doing the right thing. Alexis was pretty angry with her mom and he didn't want to put her through more than she'd already experienced but Renee had a point. She needed to spend more time around them if they were going to repair their relationship. But a part of him could give a fig about Renee getting her kids to love her again. She was the one who screwed up and walked away. Why should she get a second chance at messing with their hearts? But even as the angry thoughts scrolled through his head, he shot a look at Renee and caught the very real fear in her eyes that her girls might never forgive her, and he realized she was probably beating herself up more than he ever could.

Unsure of how he really felt and not particularly interested in digging to find out, he grunted something else in the way of goodbye and headed out to the stables. Working with horses was something he knew and understood. He'd just stick with that.

RENEE WATCHED AS JOHN STALKED off and seeing as she wasn't entirely sure if he'd just told her to get off his property or go ahead and enjoy an iced tea, she decided to seek out the girls before she returned to town. He hadn't agreed to her offer but he hadn't expressly turned her down, either. Renee chose to think optimistically. Perhaps she could get Gladys on her side. Going to the house, she hesitated at the front door, wondering if she should knock or just go in. Deciding it was best to proceed with caution, she gave the door a soft knock and waited.

She could hear the laughter of her girls, at least Taylor, and Renee smiled. Taylor was always her most exuberant child. A tomboy with a wild nest of blond hair that was stick straight and likely to be standing on end each morning. Renee used to fight with her, trying to get a brush through that mess. Tears sprang to her eyes as the memory of being with her girls every day—before she made the decision to leave—made her stiffen against the bittersweet moment. She was different now and she'd never be the woman she was then. Her fingers strayed to the badge on her jacket and as the pads grazed the hard metal, she sought strength from within and from God. She had just enough time to suck a deep breath of cleansing air before the door opened and Taylor stood there.

"Hi, sweetheart," Renee said, fighting the urge to sweep the little girl into her arms. "Can I come in and visit for a bit?"

"I have to ask Grammy Stemmy," Taylor said solemnly before running from the door. Renee stepped over the threshold and could hear Taylor yelling in the kitchen. "Renee is here. Can she come in and visit?"

Fresh pain spiked through Renee as her child referred to her by name as if she were a stranger. No doubt Alexis had a hand in that. The girls would do whatever their older sister told them and right now Alexis was more than willing to sever any tie to their mother. But Renee was tougher than that and she was *still* their mother, no matter what they called her.

"I suppose," Gladys said warily, wiping her hands on a dish towel. "We were just about to have some hot cider and cherry turnovers. Would you like to share some with us?"

"Sounds wonderful. Thank you."

Renee followed Gladys around to the kitchen and took a seat at the expansive oak table, noting that the two little girls clambered into seats right beside her but Alexis was nowhere to be seen. Disappointed that her eldest daughter was purposefully avoiding her, she focused on the joy at having her little girls flocked around her. As she accepted a small plate with a pastry from Gladys, she started casual conversation.

"Are you excited about starting school, Taylor?"

Taylor's expression dissolved into a mutinous scowl even as she chewed on her turnover. "I hate school."

"How do you know that, sweetheart? You've never been to school yet. Besides, it's only kindergarten. I bet you'll have a wonderful time and make lots of new friends."

"I don't want friends. I want to work with the horses and Mr. John."

"Well, I'm sure Mr. John loves your help with the horses but he wouldn't want you to miss out on school. He knows how important it is."

"Yeah, I guess. Daddy never made us go to school. He said school never did him any good so why should he make us go?"

Renee burned inside at Jason's stupid statement and wondered how in the hell she ever considered him the love of her life. Struggling with her answer, she smiled and said in the nicest way she could muster, "Uh, sometimes Daddy didn't know what he was talking about. School is very important and I think you're going to love it."

"Why?" Taylor's bell-like voice tinkled softly as she suddenly looked intrigued. "Do they have horses at school?"

"Not that I'm aware but they have libraries with lots of books that they will let you check out for free and then you can read all about horses."

Taylor seemed to consider this but suddenly her face screwed into a frown. "I don't know how to read," she said.

"All the more reason to go to school. Your teacher will teach you how to read and then you can read anything you like. But in the meantime, before you learn to read, they have what's called picture books and I'll bet there are picture books devoted completely to horses. Would you like to see pictures of pretty horses?"

"There's no prettier horse than Mr. John's Cisco. He's very pretty but you can't get too close to him because he's been spooked by a bad person."

"Spooked?" Renee asked.

"Yeah, Mr. John works with horses that are sad or mean 'cuz someone wasn't nice to them. And Cisco is my favorite."

Renee was mildly impressed in spite of herself. She had to admit she had a soft spot for abused animals, as well. "What does Cisco look like?"

Taylor flung her arms as wide as they would go. "He's bigger than this and real tall. Mr. John said he's seventeen hands but I don't know what that means. I think it means he's like a giant 'cuz he is."

"He sounds very big," Renee agreed, returning to the subject of school. "So, you think you might be willing to check out school then, if we can find some horse picture books?"

Taylor nodded. "Maybe I'll go just to check out this library thing. But I'm not making promises that I'll like school."

"Absolutely. No promises." Renee smiled and suddenly remembered something. Opening her purse, she pulled out Mr. BunBun. The moment Taylor saw what was in Renee's hand, her eyes widened and she clasped her hands tightly as her voice hit a high-pitched squeal of delight that felt like heaven against Renee's ears despite its ear-drum shattering quality.

"Mr. BunBun!" Taylor hugged the bedraggled stuffed animal to her small chest and nearly squeezed the stuffing out of it in her excitement. "How'd you find him?"

"When I was looking for you girls I found the house you were living in with your dad and Mr. BunBun was all by himself. I knew you would miss him so I grabbed him before leaving."

"Thank you so much!" Taylor said and impulsively kissed Renee's cheek.

Chloe, watching her sister, copied the gesture and Renee received a sloppy kiss from her youngest daughter. Unable to help herself, Renee scooped both girls into a tight embrace, her heart cracking from the unparalleled joy cascading through her body. The girls giggled and Renee smiled through her tears. The moment was nearly perfect. She only wished Alexis were there in the cuddle. Seconds later, Renee's unspoken wish was granted—albeit not in the way she'd been hoping.

"What are you doing?" Alexis's imperious tone cut through the happy moment as easily as a hot knife through butter and the girls scattered.

Taylor held up her rabbit. "Renee brought me Mr. BunBun," she said, though her chastised tone scraped on Renee's nerves. Alexis shouldn't make her sisters feel bad for showing affection to their mother. Taylor moved farther away from Renee and Chloe followed.

Renee caught Gladys's watchful stare as the scene unfolded. Standing, Renee met her daughter's hot gaze and knew the moment was now or never to remind her daughter that she was still their mother. "Alexis Janelle Dolling, you will not speak to your sisters that way," Renee said, knowing she was likely digging the hole even deeper between the two of them but she couldn't stand by and watch as Alexis bullied the girls. "We were having a lovely moment until you came in and started glaring at the girls for even being near me. That will stop right now."

"You can't tell me what to do." Alexis sneered, but her eyes welled with moisture. "And you're not our mother anymore. You stopped being our mother the day you walked out on us."

"I made a terrible mistake. I admit that. I will gladly spend the rest of my life making up for it but that doesn't mean that you can talk to me or your sisters so disrespectfully."

"We don't want to hear your excuses," Alexis said. "And Taylor left behind that dumb stuffed animal for a reason. It's trash. Isn't it, Taylor?" She looked pointedly at Taylor until Taylor's bottom lip trembled as she struggled to let her precious bunny go a second time. Renee was shocked at the level of Alexis's anger that she'd be willing to sacrifice Taylor's feelings for her own spite.

Renee stopped Taylor from dropping the bunny to the table, and ignoring Alexis for a moment, tucked a wayward strand of white-blond hair behind Taylor's ear as she said softly, "Sweetheart, you don't have to give up Mr. BunBun. He's your special bunny and only you can decide when it's time to let him go. Okay?"

Taylor nodded slowly and clutched the bunny tightly. Looking to Alexis she said, "He's not trash!" and ran from the room.

Sensing the tension, Chloe started to cry and out of instinct Renee scooped the toddler into her arms. Alexis reacted violently, running to Renee and trying to jerk Chloe out of her arms. Renee twisted so that Chloe wasn't accidentally hurt in the process and suddenly John was there, plucking Alexis up as if she weighed nothing and placing her firmly away from Renee.

Renee realized as she soothed Chloe that John must've been watching the scene from the hallway.

"Alexis," he said, commanding her daughter's attention as angry tears streamed down her face. "Never attack your mother like that. That's not okay in this house. You could've hurt someone, especially your sister. Do you understand?"

She nodded jerkily but Renee caught a nasty look just the same.

"Can you apologize?" he asked and she shook her head. As if understanding, he patted her on the shoulder and said, "All right then, go on to your room and think about what you're so riled up about and maybe we can talk about it later."

"I don't want her here," Alexis said in a low tone. "Please make her leave."

At that Renee felt a section of her heart splinter and fall to pieces. Her daughter hated her and that would probably never change. Tears blinded her as she pressed a kiss to Chloe's head and handed her to John. "I'll see you tomorrow morning," she said, then added to Alexis, "I'm not leaving you girls ever again. That's a promise. You can be mad for as long as you want but that's not going to change the fact that I love you, Alexis. And deep down, you love me, too."

CHAPTER SIX

JOHN RESISTED THE URGE to follow Renee out but his eyes tracked her progress as she drove out of the driveway.

He caught Gladys's watchful stare and he couldn't help the scowl that followed. "Don't start thinking there's more to this than there is. There's no rule that says I can't feel bad for the woman for the mess she's created. I'm human, too."

"Oh, stop your blathering. I never said anything. But no matter what you say I think it was right decent of you to come to her rescue when Alexis flew at her like that. I think her heart just about broke when Alexis reacted that way."

"Yeah. I saw that. Think I should talk to Alexis?"

Gladys considered it for a moment and then shook her head. "No. I'd let her work through it on her own. She's got a deep well full of misery to deal with and we don't need to heap more on her plate. Besides, I think you got your point across pretty good. If she doesn't show up for dinner maybe you ought to check in on her but until then, let's just give her some space."

John heaved a private sigh of relief. He didn't know how to console an angry little girl but he hated to see her so upset.

"She has a long road ahead of her with that child," Gladys commented as she packaged the remaining turnovers. "I don't envy her."

"That makes two of us," he agreed. "You think she can change?"

Gladys shrugged. "Time will tell but I'm not holding my breath at the moment. She's got to adjust that attitude of hers or else she's just going to spin her wheels with Alexis."

John glanced away, voicing his private thoughts on the subject. "There's no excuse for leaving your family behind."

"You're right about that and I know you know what that's all about. Did you ever forgive your father for leaving?"

"No."

Gladys chuckled. "Didn't think so. Like I said, that woman's got a rough row to hoe but in the meantime, we'll be there to catch the girls before they fall this time around."

He shifted, hating how he'd somehow, unwittingly, wandered into emotional territory. Gladys was a tricky one. Always had been. Probably why she and his mom had been such tight friends. They were peas in a pod. She prodded at him and he emitted a low groan as her point went straight home. "I'd be a liar if I said I've never said or done anything I regret," he admitted in a tight voice. "But I don't understand how a mother could leave her babies. Gladys, I don't think I'll *ever* understand and if *I* can't understand how is that little girl going to?"

"No one is asking you to figure things out for her. She's a smart kid. She'll do that on her own. But," Gladys sighed as if hating to agree with Renee on anything, and then said, "in the meantime, she needs to be around her mother."

"Renee suggested I hire her for help around the house with the girls. Said you were too old."

Gladys chuckled. "That woman's got spunk, I'll give her that. But as much as I hate to admit it, these old bones are feeling the years piling up behind them," she admitted grudgingly. "I could use a hand around here. Chloe is a handful even though she's sweeter than freshly churned butter and I think she would love to have her mama around. She doesn't remember her very well and she harbors the least amount of piss and vinegar. I think it would be smart for Renee to start rebuilding with Chloe first. I'll be here to smooth out the rough spots but she's right. I am a bit long in the tooth to be chasing after a toddler while the other girls are in school."

John heaved a heavy sigh and nodded. "I guess I could fix up the guesthouse. Although I hate the idea of harboring that woman on my property," he added with a glower. "Frankly, if it weren't something the girls probably need to get over this mess, I'd tell her to pound sand. I don't give a shit about her feelings in this."

"What about the court stuff?"

"Oh, Sheriff Casey isn't going to make a stink over anything as long as those girls are safe and happy. Besides, the order doesn't say anything about Renee keeping her distance or anything. I suppose as long as everyone is happy, no one needs to be the wiser."

"So it's settled, then? Renee is moving in?" Gladys's mouth firmed, no more happy about it than John but willing to see it through for the girls' sake just like him.

"I suppose she is." He walked from the kitchen, his pace brisk, but not even his quickened step could keep him from the realization that he was about to invite more complications into his life and if the warning tingle in his gut was any indication, he might've just changed his life forever

RENEE WALKED WITH TAYLOR'S hand firmly in her own as Alexis practically jogged three steps ahead with John and Chloe somewhere in between.

"I don't want you walking me to class," Alexis declared, looking pointedly at Renee before continuing with strong purposeful steps toward the entrance.

Renee looked down at Taylor. "How about you?"

"You can walk me to class if you want to, I suppose," Taylor answered. "You can show me where these picture books are that you were talking about."

"Deal."

The school was an old brick building with a bell at the top, a remnant of when the school was first built in the late 1800s, and it looked right out of an episode of *Little House on the Prairie*.

"Do you think that bell still works?" Taylor asked.

"I don't know but we can ask your teacher," Renee said, smiling.

She glanced up at John and wondered if this was where he went to school. He seemed to know his way around well enough as they went straight to the front office and a few people even nodded in surprise at seeing him there.

"Old school chums?" Renee surmised once she'd caught up to him.

"I guess you could say that," John answered, but didn't elaborate further. Talk about a man of little words. If he strung together more than two sentences in a row she'd fall over in shock. Grumbling to herself, she kept the rest of her annoyed thoughts silent as the principal greeted them.

"John Murphy? I haven't seen you in awhile but I do know you don't have kids. Who do I have the pleasure of meeting?"

Before John could answer, Renee piped in, saying, "They're mine. We're just staying with John at the ranch for now. Renee Dolling, pleased to meet you, Mr.…."

"Curtis Meany," he answered with a broad smile, coming forward to envelope her hand in a firm hand-shake. "Don't let the name fool you, I'm really a softie at heart. If I'm not careful these students run all over me. Are you from around here? I don't recall the name."

"No, we're new." Renee smiled and left it at that.

She didn't want to go into details and ruin this nice man's impression of her. It was hard enough dealing with John much less another judgmental local. "My girls, Alexis and Taylor, are starting classes today."

"Yes, here are their teachers' names and classroom numbers. If you have any questions or concerns, my door is always open. Good to see you again, John."

"Curt." John inclined his head and then gesturing for the paper in Renee's hand, said, "Let's get this show on the road. I have a horse coming in an hour."

"You can go if you like," Renee offered and was mildly surprised when he frowned in response. "If you're in a hurry…"

"I didn't say that."

"You implied."

He started to say something but then thought better of it and snapped his mouth shut. "Perhaps I did."

Renee smiled down at Taylor. "Let's go find your teacher, shall we?"

She didn't wait for John nor did she try to convince Alexis to let her walk her to class, as well. She knew her daughter well enough to know any attempt at this point would be rudely rebuffed. She'd have to let Alexis come to her. She fought back a well of fear when she considered the very real possibility that that day might never come and instead focused on the happy start she was being granted with her middle daughter.

JOHN WATCHED AS RENEE LED Taylor to her new classroom. To look at them one would never guess their circumstances. Renee looked every part the doting mother, her eyes fairly shone with love and adoration that John was almost apt to believe, if not for the reminder of Renee's defection standing beside him wearing a fierce scowl.

"She seems to be trying," John noted, almost to himself but it was really directed toward Alexis. She took the bait quite readily.

Alexis snorted. "My mom used to want to be an actress. You shouldn't believe a word she says. She's a good liar." And then she adjusted her pack and stomped in the direction of her new classroom.

An actress? It shocked him but then again…it didn't. She was sure pretty enough to fill a big screen. That blond-hair-blue-eye combination was a killer. Not to mention those curves… John shifted on the balls of his feet wondering where his mind was going and who gave it permission to wander like that.

Renee returned a short time later, a warm glow suffusing her expression that was nearly contagious.

"She settled in all right?" he asked.

"Yeah. I think she's going to have fun. Taylor has an adventurous spirit. She's game for anything that can hook her interest. But then you've probably already figured that out about her."

He had. It was one of Taylor's more endearing qualities. "She's got a sharp mind. I think school will be a good challenge for her."

Renee nodded and they walked out the front doors. The children quickly dispersed as they ran to their individual classes when the bell rang. Once at their vehicles, John climbed into his truck and then stopped to call out to Renee.

"Yeah?" she asked, her brow furrowing subtly as she regarded him warily.

"If you're still interested in the job, I suppose it's available."

"You're saying that you're willing to hire me to help out with my kids?" There was a sparkle in her eyes that he couldn't help but catch and it made him bite back what he might've said to her clever comment. She didn't give him a chance to rescind the offer and quickly jumped. "Sounds perfect. When can I move in?"

John startled at the gooseflesh that rioted up and down his arm. He swallowed. *Moving in.* It created a wealth of imagery that made his heartbeat thud painfully. Scowling, he said, "Since you're in an all-fired hurry, I suppose Friday is fine."

"Friday?" Her expression fell. "But it's only Monday. I was hoping—"

"I know what you were hoping but the guesthouse won't be ready for anyone until then. It's the soonest I can accommodate you into my schedule. It should go without saying that I still have a job to do and it doesn't include making room for yet another Dolling. You get me? Take it or leave it."

He winced privately at how surly he sounded. Damn, if he didn't sound like a cantankerous old fart but she rubbed him the wrong way in the *worst* way.

She had no business looking the way she did and coming around as if she was pretending to care when John knew full well she hadn't cared when it mattered to those little girls. Right? *Ah, great. Talking to yourself now,* he mentally chastised himself. John's lips pressed against one another and he figured that was the smartest thing he could do at this point—keep his damn mouth shut.

"Friday, 8 a.m. sharp. Don't be late." He slammed the truck door, eager to get the hell away from her and his confused thoughts.

CHAPTER SEVEN

RENEE RETURNED TO THE HOTEL, her mind buzzing and her heart full of hope for the future. Taylor was the key to breaching the wall Alexis had built around them. She didn't blame Alexis for her attitude even if it hurt. Of all the kids, Alexis remembered many details that were lost to Taylor and unknown to Chloe. Renee rubbed her palm across her stinging eyes and fought back the bad memories that always threatened to surface when she wasn't being vigilant enough.

The fights. The screaming. And the alcohol. Always a lot of that around the Dolling house. It became her way of coping with a failed life and living with a man she didn't love any longer. She'd had such big dreams as a kid. But Jason Dolling had been persuasive and her hormones had been listening. She couldn't regret everything that happened during their life together. Her girls were the shining example that even when everything else was going to shit, there was always something to be grateful for.

She wished she could take every bad memory from her daughter's mind but that wasn't an option. All she could do was be there and promise their lives would be different. And that was something she could do without reservation.

Getting sober hadn't been the easiest thing in the world but she'd had really solid motivation. She never tried to compare her journey to that of others because they're never the same or even comparable. Renee had definitely come to appreciate that old saying, Never judge a man until you've walked a mile in his shoes, because when she'd made the decision to get sober at first it was natural to assume others had it easier or harder, take your pick, but she'd learned quickly not to judge. She'd seen lawyers and doctors sitting side by side with drug addicts and no one had it easy.

She'd been no different—and no worse.

But to explain to a child the reasons why her mother left…were there words in the English language that would ever convey the reason in a way a child would understand? Renee didn't know but she desperately wanted to find out. Alexis was her soldier, her first born. She'd bonded to that girl from the moment she came screaming into the world, her lusty squall a balm to Renee's young heart, the calm in the storm that surrounded her and Jason.

Taylor was the let's-try-and-save-the-marriage baby. And by the time Chloe arrived…well, the marriage had been over before she was conceived. Yet, Renee had stayed. Drinking her failure away with her two solid friends, Jack Daniels and Jim Beam and the occasional visit by Captain Morgan on holidays.

So many bad choices. A lifetime, really. Was she poised at the precipice of yet another bad Renee Dolling decision? She just wanted her kids back so they could get back to their lives.

But then what? Her chest tightened with panic and uncertainty. She'd been so focused on finding the girls she didn't actually have a plan as to where they'd go from there. Renee's mother had always called her flighty. So far, she hadn't proven the woman wrong and the time was past to do so. Her mother had long since written her off as a daughter. So now she only had herself and her children to prove something to.

But it was enough. She wouldn't let the girls down. That was a promise. Friday couldn't come soon enough in her book.

JOHN SPENT MOST OF THE MORNING working with a skittish mare that'd been brought the day before and he was thankful for the hard work. The moment he entered the arena, she shied away, stomping the ground with her front hooves as if daring him to get closer so she could stamp a nice U-shaped mark on his forehead. He let her settle down but didn't leave the arena. He let her know that he wasn't going anywhere but didn't try connecting the lead rope to her halter, either. The two eyed each other and John settled into a comfortable space inside his head. He could sense her distrust and knew this girl would take considerable work on his part to get her to the point where she didn't try to kill anyone who came near her.

As it was it took four men to unload her into the horse paddock and she'd shown her displeasure by kicking the shit out of the stable gate as she tried to get out of her stall. Her wild screams told him she didn't like enclosed spaces and he soon moved her to a bigger, much roomier stall that he usually reserved for foaling mares. Luckily, at the moment he didn't need the special sized stall. Once she didn't feel the walls closing in on her, she settled with an uneasy whinny but none of the ranch hands wanted to go near her. John didn't blame them. He instructed everyone to steer clear of the young mare appropriately named Vixen and so far they had. Today was the first day he'd had the chance to formerly introduce himself so to speak and by the murderous glint in her eye, the introduction wasn't going so well.

"You and I are going to get along just fine," he said low and soft as if the horse could understand every word. "I know you've had a hard time of it but no one is going to hurt you here. You have to behave, though, you hear me? No more kicking stable doors and scaring the life out of my ranch hands. I don't pay them enough for that shit."

Vixen tossed her head as if to say "that's your problem" and he chuckled softly. That it was. "We're going to get along just fine, aren't we?" he asked, a small grin lifting the corners of his mouth. There was nothing he enjoyed more than a challenge and judging by the proud and stubborn toss of the young mare's head, he'd found a damn good one.

Vixen reminded him of Alexis—all spit and fire—if only to draw attention away from the wound inside. He knew Alexis cried at night when she thought no one could hear her, when her sisters were fast asleep and she thought he was crashed out in front of the fire. But he heard her heartbroken sobs clear as if she were curled in his lap soaking his shoulder. And he'd be a liar if he didn't admit it hit him hard. But what did he know about consoling a little girl's broken heart? How was he supposed to help her heal? He was out of his league. You didn't ask a horseman to wrestle with alligators because it wasn't his specialty and he was likely to get his hand chomped off. That's how he felt. Caged with an alligator with nothing but a lead rope and a prayer. By his estimation, neither one was going to do much good.

So where did that leave him? The mare stared warily, watching and waiting for his next move, and the answer came to him with the slow cumbersome gearshift of the truly reluctant. The only way Alexis was going to heal was if she had her mama back in her life, which meant, and he really didn't like the sound of this, he was going to have to help Renee mend the fence.

And that meant playing nice with the woman.

Aww hell.

He didn't know how to do that, either.

He glanced back at Vixen, who nickered—or maybe it was a snicker—and said with a shake of his head and a promise in his eye, "Oh, don't look so smug. You're next, hot hooves. You're about the *only* thing I know how to handle around here. So, let's get to work, shall we?"

RENEE GLARED AT THE SKY and cursed the snow spiral- ing out of the dark, ominous clouds as she wrestled another box out of her car and struggled to keep her footing on the slippery ground.

"Here, let me take that before you land face-first in a snowdrift," John said gruffly, lifting the box from her arms before she could protest. "We could've waited until Monday, after the storm passed us by," he said over his shoulder as she hurried to catch up.

"No, I've waited long enough to be around my girls. I'm not letting some— Oh!" She slipped a little and nearly landed on her rear but somehow caught herself before doing so. John didn't slow nor did he glance back at her. Straightening, she took more care as she made her way toward the guesthouse. "I'm not going to let some storm get in my way. Besides, who's to say this storm would be over by then? No way. I'm settling in and getting comfortable as soon as possible."

He turned abruptly and she almost ran into him. "Oh! You should say something before you do that!" she admonished with a glare, her breath pluming in a misty curl between them. "The ground is hard enough to walk without you stopping for no good reason in the middle of the path. Have you ever considered putting in a nice sidewalk to the guesthouse?"

"No. That would encourage people to stay longer

than they're welcome," he answered, shifting the box easily although Renee knew it was heavy. So there must be some muscles hidden beneath that flannel shirt she noted with a private shrug. Big deal. She'd never been one to swoon over some hunky cowboy type. Wrangler butts don't drive *her* nuts. Good thing, too, because a cursory, almost defiant sweep of his butt, revealed an ass that she couldn't help but admit was on the perfect side. He caught her unfortunate perusal and his eyebrow lifted only so slightly as he said, "Flattered but not interested. The house is the only thing available in this deal."

The nerve of this guy! As if she'd be interested in him. The idea bordered on ridiculous. Pulling the box from him and grunting only slightly from the effort, she said coolly, "I wasn't inquiring. I can handle the rest, thank you. What else did you have to say when you nearly made me run into you?"

She expected him to fight her over the box but he didn't. The jerk merely shrugged and pulled a key from his pocket, saying, "I was just going to mention that you can help yourself to the woodshed out back and I suggest you build a fire right away. It's the only source of heat in there. Here's the key." And then after pushing the key into the lock since her hands were full, he walked away, not slipping even once although Renee was really hoping he would—it would serve him right—and disappeared in the direction of the barn.

Nerve, nerve, nerve! The man had it in spades. Oh,

sure, he gave off that quiet, unassuming vibe but the man actually had an ego the size of…well, for lack of anything more witty or clever, *Texas!*

She managed to hold on to the box and open the door with a minimal amount of swearing and despite the bone-chilling cold was actually sweating from the exertion.

Dropping the box with less delicacy than she should've, she winced as she heard the muffled crack of something breaking and wondered which of her precious few possessions she'd just shattered. After huffing a short breath and vowing to open the box later to find out, she decided to wander the small house to see what she was looking at as far as living conditions go.

Well, it was better than her hotel room, she noted after a quick perusal of the small house. One bedroom, one bathroom, a kitchenette and a tiny living room. Not bad.

If only it weren't wallpapered with some kind of hideous rose wallpaper that looked like it was taken straight out of the pages of a Sears, Roebuck catalog, circa 1920. She grimaced. Thank God she wasn't planning on staying long. This wallpaper might make her lose her mind. She peered out the small front window. Nothing but more snow fluttered from the sky, threatening to bury the small house and the ranch itself if the storm didn't let up. Flicking the living room light on, she pushed the box out of the way of traffic and readied herself for another trip to the car. She didn't have much but at the moment, even one more trip outside wasn't a pleasant thought. Get on with it, she chided herself, wrapping her shawl more tightly around her neck. If she didn't want to sleep in her jeans tonight, she'd better get the rest of her stuff before the path from the driveway to the guesthouse became damn near impassable.

Trudging through the gathering snow, her toes freezing in her worn hiking boots, she couldn't help the quick glance toward the barn as she wondered what kind of woman—if any—would turn John Murphy's head.

Likely as not, that woman didn't exist. She scowled at her thoughts.

Yeah, well, who cares? It's not like she was hoping to be that woman, anyway. She just wanted her kids back. End of story.

Besides, no one in their right mind would want to live here, she thought with a surly temper as she sank to her knee in fresh powder and nearly toppled forward in a frontal snow angel dive. Pulling her foot free, she muttered with a fierce glower, "I hate snow. I really, really, *really* hate snow." *And I think I just might hate you, too, John Murphy.*

CHAPTER EIGHT

THE STORM DIDN'T LET UP as John had thought and since there was little work he could do with the horses in the current weather, all he could do was wait it out. Normally, he'd just tinker around the house, doing odd jobs he'd put off but he couldn't turn around without stumbling over a little girl underfoot since Alexis and Taylor had been given a snow day.

Peering toward the guesthouse, he was satisfied to see that the little chimney was pumping out smoke, which meant Renee, despite the odds he was betting to the contrary, knew how to build a fire. At least she wouldn't freeze. Not that he was worried.

He moved to the living room and thought about reading the local paper he'd missed from the previous week but as he entered the room it was hard to avoid the long, sullen faces of three little girls who were dying from boredom.

Earlier Renee had found an old puzzle and she and Taylor had spent an hour putting it together only to discover it was missing a piece. But Taylor had just giggled and Renee's expression of pure joy had been hard to walk by without taking notice. He could see the happiness shining from her eyes at her daughter's carefree laughter and it jerked his foundation a little. Alexis, of course, had had nothing to do with her mother or her invitation to join them. For a split second John regretted seeing the light dimming in Renee's eyes at her daughter's open rejection and it had bothered him that he cared. Later, Renee had returned to her cottage and the girls had slowly slipped into terminal boredom when Gladys had taken to her bed early.

It was one thing to be locked in a house of your own with your own things to keep you company, but it was completely something else when you're locked in a stranger's house with nothing familiar.

He remembered what he and Evan used to do when the snow piled high and their mom had had enough of their tussling in the house. She sent them outside in the snow with the order to stay out of trouble or else.

A speculative glance toward the girls had his mind moving. If memory served, there was still a toboggan in the attic gathering dust along with the rest of his childhood mementos. He'd be willing to bet Taylor would love a ride down the hill on that thing.

A few minutes later, he entered the living room with an announcement.

"Bundle up, we're going outside."

"It's snowing," Alexis said.

"Are you going to melt if a snowflake lands on you?"

She scowled. "No. But it's cold outside and Chloe's still sick."

"Fresh air never hurt anyone. Besides, her cough is getting better by the day. Discussion over. Go get dressed and help your sisters, please. We're going outside."

Alexis didn't argue further but the unhappy pout told him volumes about her disposition. He didn't let it get to him, though. He suspected her attitude had less to do with the snow and more to do with the fact he'd let her mama move into the guesthouse. He withheld a sigh. Despite some reservations, he supposed he had to find a way to get those two talking again. He glanced at the small guesthouse, and figured he might as well stop putting it off and start lending a hand. To that end, he made a decision that he hoped didn't blow up in his face.

"I'll be right back," he told the girls who were in the process of being bundled into new jackets and mittens that had been part of the back-to-school shopping spree that he'd instructed Gladys to make. He had to admit, Gladys had a better eye when it came to girly stuff than he did. His idea of high fashion was a clean flannel shirt but, shoot, the horses didn't care what he wore. "Make sure you zipper up good. The wind is blowing a bit," he instructed.

"Maybe we should stay in the house then," Alexis muttered but continued to help Taylor into her mittens.

Making his way to the guesthouse, he gave the door a short rap. A minute later Renee appeared wearing a pink fuzzy sweater that plunged at the neckline in an enticing V, practically plucking John's eyeballs from his head and nestling them between her ample breasts, until she crossed her arms at the immediate chill to ask, "Is everything okay?"

Uh. Shaking off the odd spell—had she been wearing that sweater earlier? Seemed funny that he just now noticed how much it flattered her figure—he focused on her face as he answered. "We're going sledding. Do you want to come?"

"Sledding?" She blinked at him, her mouth working silently as she considered the offer. "You mean actual sledding? Down a hill or something?"

"That's generally how it's done. You've never gone sledding before?"

"No. I didn't grow up around the snow," she answered, tightening her arms and scowling much like Alexis did. "It's not a childhood requirement, you know."

"You're right," he agreed amiably. "So, here's your chance to see what you've been missing. Bundle up and meet us out front."

He didn't give her much opportunity to say more and he did that purposefully. He was having a hard time focusing when his eyeballs wanted to slide downward to enjoy the view that shouldn't have interested him at all given their situation. But, as his brother liked to point out with a cheeky grin, he had needs, too. He shook off the immediate bells and whistles that hooted and hollered in his head at the thought of satisfying those pent-up needs with Renee Dolling and walked a little faster away from the small house.

The girls, stamping their feet in the snow and blowing little clouds in the frosty air, gaped at the toboggan he carried under his arm.

"What's that, Mr. John?" Taylor asked, her smart gaze feasting on the long, sturdy contraption that despite its age was in excellent shape.

"It's a toboggan and we're going to do something that I used to do with my brother, Evan, back when we were kids and there was nothing to do but watch the snow fall. Come with me." Bending, he scooped Chloe up, carrying the toddler while pulling the toboggan behind him, his own breath making blue-gray puffs that quickly disappeared in the frigid air. Out of the corner of his eye he caught sight of Renee running to catch up. He kept his expression neutral though he had the strange impulse to grin.

Taylor squealed and jumped into a snowdrift, giggling as the white powder swallowed her small frame until she had to kick her feet to regain her footing. "I like snow," she announced as Renee took her hand and pulled her out. "Do you like snow?" she inquired and John listened a little more intently for Renee's answer.

"I like being with you girls," Renee answered diplomatically and John chuckled softly. She was breathing a little harder from the exertion and her cheeks bloomed prettily, not that she needed any help in that department, John noted with exasperation. Renee tried making small talk with Alexis and John admired her tenacity in the face of her daughter's dark expression. "Remember that time we went to Kirkwood and—"

"No. I don't."

Alexis trudged ahead, her arms swinging with the effort as she put distance between them all. John heard Renee's unhappy sigh and slowed his own gait so they were walking side by side.

"She's pretty headstrong," he said, needing to say something that might put Alexis's rejection into perspective.

"Always has been. But she used to be on my side," Renee said. "She's not the kind of kid who forgives or forgets easily."

"Would you want her to be?"

"No. Not really. I've always felt that Alexis had a good head on her shoulders. That life wouldn't tip her over like it did me. She's always had the uncanny ability to see through the bullshit. I wish I'd had that talent when I was young."

John wondered at that statement. He was slowly beginning to realize that Renee's past may well be a chaotic one. Shrugging, he said, "She'll come around."

"I know. But it hurts to be on the outside."

"Give it some time. She's still getting used to having you around again. But she misses her mama and that's the truth."

Renee looked at him sharply. "Really? Did she say something?"

"Not in words. It's a feeling. A hunch."

Her expression fell and she sniffed. "Forgive me if

I don't put much store in hunches and feelings. My daughter hates me and goes out of her way to make sure I feel the sting of it every day. I would've been more hopeful if she'd actually admitted something to you."

"You don't always get what you want the way that you want it. Hasn't anyone ever told you that?" He cocked his head at her, while Chloe tried to catch snowflakes. Renee smiled at Chloe but gave him a hard look.

"Of course I know that. I'm just saying—"

"And so am I."

Silence stretched between them as they both processed what'd been said, and just as John was thinking he'd said too much and perhaps should've kept his opinion to himself, they arrived at the small hill John had had in mind.

"Are you sure it's safe?" Renee asked, peering anxiously down the gentle slope as John put Chloe on her feet near her sisters. "I mean, it looks a little steep for the girls."

John chuckled. "Chloe could go down this hill by herself. I'll set up the track and then we'll take turns taking the girls down. Okay? It's completely safe. I promise." And then he gave her a wide—almost daring—grin. Why? He hadn't a clue but her reaction was worth the confusion.

RENEE FELT A SUBTLE JUMP in her heartrate at the smile playing on John's lips and her imagination kicked into overdrive at the worst moment. Pulling her gaze away with obvious effort, she glanced back down the hill and then at her girls. "All right...I guess that'd be okay. How are you going to make the track?"

"That's part of the fun. I'll pave the way so that when we go down with the girls, we have something to stick to. Sort of like a road."

She didn't have a clue as to what he was talking about but she was willing to watch and see. "Be my guest, road master. Carry on. We'll sit back and watch as you crack your head open."

John's bark of laughter surprised her and she smiled in spite of herself. "Watch and learn, city girl," he said.

Were they—*good Lord*—almost flirting with each other?

Maybe a tad, a small voice answered, encouraging her to continue playing, which she obliged with little resistance.

"You say that like it's a bad thing," she retorted, her smile growing, then gestured. "We're waiting..."

"Right. Step aside, females. Watch the Toboggan King work his magic."

Renee laughed, enjoying seeing this different side of the man she swore she'd never like, and picked up Chloe. "I hope my cell phone works out here," she said to her youngest daughter in a conspiratorial tone. "Because I sure as hell can't carry him if he goes and breaks himself."

John looked back at her. "Ye of little faith..."

Chloe giggled and pointed as John positioned himself on the sled at the top of the hill and shoved off.

Renee gasped as he skimmed the snow and left behind a sleek trail that looked smooth as ice before slowing to a stop at the bottom, safe and sound and grinning from ear to ear.

Oh, he shouldn't do that. Who knew there was a Colgate smile—blindingly white—hidden behind that stern scowl? It was as if she were seeing him for the first time and that was patently ridiculous but, hey, it was the truth and she was never much of a liar, anyway. Million watt. Straight, white teeth. What a killer smile. A lady killer, that is. She drew a shaky breath, fitted a tremulous smile to her own lips and tried to let the moment of insanity fade without drawing too much attention to the odd flutter and quiver she was feeling on the inside.

As he trudged back up the hill, he said, "I can't believe I'd forgotten how much fun that is. Evan and I used to spend whole days crafting these amazing trails for the sled, going so far as to make jumps, too. Okay, who's next? Alexis? How about you and me? We'll show these kids how it's done."

Alexis, interest piqued in spite of her earlier bad attitude, agreed readily and climbed in front of John as he wrapped his arms around her to tuck his feet. "Hold on, this train is moving fast," he called out as the toboggan started the slow descent and quickly picked up speed.

Renee laughed at the delighted shriek Alexis let out and John's accompanying deep-throated laughter. A warmth that had nothing to do with her wool coat filled her and Renee, for a second, lost herself in the idyllic scene before her. She wondered why John never married and had a family of his own. He seemed to be a natural with kids, though at first glance she'd never have guessed by his surly attitude. John was an enigma that Renee had to admit she was fairly curious in figuring out.

Alexis and John made their way back up the hill, cheeks a ruddy pink from the cold, and for the first time since she'd seen her daughter again, she wore a smile instead of a frown. It lit up her features from within and her daughter's natural beauty transformed her young face to one that would surely break hearts someday. Renee could only hope that her daughter wouldn't make the same mistakes as she'd made, falling in love with the wrong man, giving up her hopes and dreams, and lastly, giving up on herself. Shaking off the sad thoughts, she focused on the joy of the moment and soon her spirits lifted as she watched Taylor hopping up and down. "My turn! My turn!"

"I'll go down with you," Renee volunteered, even though she was a little leery of the whole idea of flying down the hill with nothing more than her feet for brakes.

Renee settled into the back and John placed Taylor in front. With a gentle push, they started the descent, which at first was pretty sedate but then it was like being on a Disneyland thrill ride without the benefit of being strapped in. Taylor squealed in delight and within seconds Renee was doing the same.

Who knew hurtling headlong down a monster hill could be so thrilling?

"Let's go again!" Taylor exclaimed, pulling impatiently on Renee's hand as she dragged the toboggan back up the hill.

"You bet!"

And so they spent the better half of the day slipping and sliding, laughing and giggling until they were winded and exhausted and barely able to drag their bodies back to the house for some much needed hot apple cider and hot chocolate.

And Renee couldn't remember when she'd had so much fun with such an unlikely partner. She slanted a short look at John as he walked beside her, pulling the toboggan with Chloe riding on his shoulders. Maybe there was more to John Murphy than immediately met the eye.

Just maybe, she might be in a mind to find out.

CHAPTER NINE

WHILE JOHN WORKED ON the hot cider and chocolate, Renee helped the girls out of their wet and snow-caked clothing and into soft pajamas and slippers.

"These look warm," Renee observed casually of the girls' pajamas. "Did you pick these out?"

"Yep. On the 'net," Taylor said, wiggling with delight into her horse-patterned top. "Mr. John said there's no mall anywhere near here and he hates to deal with the people so Mr. John had Grammy buy our stuff on his computer."

"That was nice of him to buy you girls some pj's."

Alexis nodded but it was obvious she wasn't going to elaborate for Renee's benefit. Thankfully, Taylor wasn't exactly a locked box when it came to safe-guarding information.

"We didn't have any clothes 'cept for the ones that we was wearing the night we came and Mr. John said they weren't fit to line a dog's bed. My jeans had holes in them," Taylor said. "But now, I got lots of jeans with no holes and I love my new shoes."

Renee made a mental note to talk to John about the

purchases made thus far. It wasn't right for him to foot the bill. She'd have to find out how much he'd spent so she could make arrangements to pay him back.

But for the time being, the girls were running from the room toward the kitchen, squealing and laughing as they called out for their warm drinks.

Renee hung back a moment as she gazed about the room that her girls had taken over. It was much like the rest of the house, masculine in its decor, but somehow her girls had put their stamp on things with small accents. A Little Mermaid lamp here, a pink throw blanket tossed casually on the bed over there, and lots of clothes strewn about that were certainly the sign of little girl territory. It was the nicest place they'd ever lived and it hurt that Renee hadn't been the one to provide it for them.

Smoothing the wrinkles from the comforter, she wondered if John would let her buy some girly sheets for their bed. But as soon as the thought crossed her mind, she discarded it. There was no sense in buying sheets for a bed they were only going to be in temporarily. Swallowing a sigh at the fight she'd have on her hands the day the girls had to say goodbye to the ranch and to their Mr. John, Renee shelved the unhappy thoughts and pasted a bright smile on her lips for her daughters' benefit.

They weren't leaving today. Her aunt used to tell her, don't borrow trouble from tomorrow when there was happiness to be found in today.

Good advice, Renee realized, for she really didn't want to think about that day, either.

LATER THAT NIGHT, AFTER copious amounts of hot chocolate, cider, a dinner of steak and potatoes, games of Uno, and after the girls had been tucked into bed exhausted from the day's activities, John felt himself reluctant to say good-night to the one woman in the world he ought to steer clear of.

Funny how those things work.

"I guess I should turn in, too," Renee said, although she wasn't making a move toward the door just yet. He took that as a sign that she was hesitant for her own reasons and much to his shame, he jumped at it.

"Come sit a minute," he suggested, gesturing toward the crackling fire in the hearth. The dancing light threw soft shadows into the living room that offset the eerie glow from the snow-packed window. "There's no need to run off just because the girls aren't here. I don't bite."

She smiled. "Are you sure?"

"Am I sure that I don't bite or am I sure that I wouldn't mind some company?"

"Um, both."

He chuckled and followed her to the sofa. "I think the girls had a really good day and I want to thank you for making that effort for them. I get the feeling that playing in the snow isn't your idea of a good time on most days."

"It's not but I didn't realize it could be so much fun, not to mention one heck of a workout. I think muscles I never knew I had are going to be protesting tomorrow morning."

He smiled but his overactive imagination had

already snagged the opportunity to be distracting and the effort was forced. Stop thinking about her curves, he instructed his brain, searching wildly for something else to fill the space in his head. Think of taxes, the fence that needs mending—*anything!* "Tell me a bit about yourself," he suggested and she faltered, the light fading quickly from her eyes. "You don't have to. I'm just a little curious about the woman—"

"Who left her kids behind?" she interrupted sharply, moving to leave but he stopped her with a firm hand.

"No, that's not what I was going to say. Are you always in a habit of jumping to conclusions?"

She bit her lip. "Lately. I guess. What were you going to say?"

"Just that I'm curious to know more about the woman who is nothing like I thought she was."

Renee settled back on the sofa as she said, "What do you mean?"

"Well, you're a bit of a wild card, if you know what I mean. Unpredictable. What I knew about you was that you left your girls behind for reasons I don't know but then you've shown your fierce determination to get them back. To win their love. Something tells me that there's more to Renee Dolling, deep down. Tell me about that woman."

She blushed, and in the soft light with her wind-chapped lips and burnished cheeks, she bloomed into an incomparable beauty right before his eyes. He resisted the pull, the urge to sample those lips, to nibble along her collarbone and taste the silken skin, but the effort cost him.

She cleared her throat and glanced away. "You give me too much credit. I'm just a mother who made a terrible mistake who's trying to fix it. Contrary to what it may look like, my girls mean everything to me. They're all I have. I married Jason right out of high school. We were big dreamers with even bigger plans. Unfortunately, neither one of us had the wherewithal to figure out how to make those dreams a reality. And then, I got pregnant."

"So Alexis wasn't planned I take it."

"None of the girls were planned," Renee said drily. "But they were the joy of my life. I was just too…" she drew a deep breath "…too drunk most of the time to realize it."

"Drunk?" An echo of her admission in court about rehab came back to him.

She met his stare. "Yeah. Drunk. I was…I mean, I am an alcoholic. That's why I left."

He digested her admission in silence, taking a moment to let it sink in. "What did you ex-husband think about you wanting to get sober?" he asked.

She smiled without humor. "What did he think? He tried to talk me out of it. Jason was constantly trying to get me to drink because when I drank I forgot how I wanted to get away from him. I'd been trying to leave him for almost a year when I got pregnant with Chloe."

"So you were still having sex with him even though you wanted to leave…"

"That's a little personal, don't you think?" Renee's mouth hardened.

"I'm just trying to understand, you know…connect the dots," he said by way of apology.

"If you figure out my twisted path from then to now, leave a breadcrumb trail. Sometimes I still don't know how I got here," she retorted with a trace of bitterness. Then she sighed and shook her head in answer to his bold question. "No. I wasn't."

Dawning came quickly. "Chloe isn't your husband's child."

A long moment passed before Renee slowly shook her head again.

"Yet he agreed to raise her as his own?"

"He thought it would make me stay and it did…for a while. But the drinking and the fighting just got worse and worse…until the night I blacked out and woke up with a gash in my forehead and the girls crying in the backseat of my car. I'd tried to drive away with them and I was smashed."

"You're lucky you didn't kill someone."

"I know that. That's why I knew I had to leave in order to get sober. There was a rehab facility with an opening but I couldn't take the kids with me. I told Jason I had to get sober for our marriage. I lied. But it was the only way he'd agree to take care of the kids. I was in for two months and toward the end of my stay, I finally told Jason when he came for visitation that I wanted a divorce. I never expected him to split with the kids. I thought he might try to intimidate me into staying with him but when he didn't, I just assumed he agreed with me that it was over. I got out and realized they were gone. Up until that day I found them here, I'd been looking for them ever since."

"And Chloe's father?"

Shame burned in her cheeks as she answered, "Never knew him. It was a one-night stand that I barely remember."

John leaned back into the sofa and exhaled softly. It was a lot to take in. Renee admitted to her mistakes and didn't flinch from the truth even if she hated her part in it. He had to respect that even if he didn't understand.

"You should've told the judge all this," he said quietly. "It might've made a difference in the outcome."

Her mouth twisted in a sad, wry grin. "Don't you remember? I tried. He wasn't interested in hearing what I had to say. He took one look at me and wrote me off as a bad mother who abandoned her kids. Just like everyone else in this town who knows my situation, which seems like just about half the population."

Renee misconstrued his silence as condemnation and ice returned to her voice as she said, "I can't change who I was…only who I am now. If you can't deal with that, that's your problem." She rose stiffly and walked to the back door as if to leave but John wasn't ready to end the night on a sour note.

"Hold on now," he said, hurrying after her. She stopped and he could see the hurt in her eyes even though she was trying to hide it. He reached out and put his hand on the door to keep her from storming out. "There you go jumping to conclusions again. Bad habit," he murmured, distracted by the soft heave of her chest and the gentle parting of her lips as she stared up at him. He blinked away the fuzz in his brain but his thoughts were foggy from being so close to her. Damn, she smelled good—earthy and sweet, like fresh alfalfa hay on a summer day. Where was he going with that thought train? *Off track.* He paused to give himself a mental shake. "I didn't mean to rile you up," he said.

She ran the tip of her tongue along her bottom lip as if she were nervous and said, "Well, you did. Rile me up," she added with a fair amount of shake in her voice, making him wonder if she was struggling with the same odd assortment of inappropriate feelings, too. He hoped so. He'd hate to realize he was traveling a one-way street. She swallowed. "But I accept your apology," she said, lifting her chin.

Her lips were so close, her mouth so tempting…he jerked and took a step away. When he grinned, it almost hurt. "Good," he said. "It's better if we get along. For the kids."

"Where have I heard that before…" she said, but her voice was strained. "All right then. Good night."

He watched her cross to the guesthouse and waited until her door closed before he shut himself in his own bedroom, feeling oddly discontented. Jerking his shirt out from the waistband of his jeans he pulled it off and over his head to toss in the laundry basket. He'd wanted to kiss her. And yet, he knew that was a bad idea. Laying a lip-lock on the one woman who was so *not* available was pure lunacy and an exercise in futility. And he wasn't usually the kind of man who dabbled in stupid ventures.

When he was down to his boxers, he climbed into the bed and punched the pillows a few times in an attempt to fluff them more to his liking but it was really just a way to blow off steam. He wanted her. Wanted her in the worst way. He pushed at his hardened erection in annoyance. Down, boy. Nothing happening for you.

Think taxes, mending fence—yeah, that didn't work the first time around, and it didn't work now. He turned onto his stomach, grimacing at the discomfort from his groin and closed his eyes, determined to put the whole incident behind him and just go to sleep.

And it almost worked. But just as he hovered between asleep and awake, Renee floated into his mental theater and instead of wearing a look of uncertainty, she smiled suggestively over her shoulder and beckoned for him to come to her as her robe parted and slid to the floor in a discarded heap.

He drifted into slumber on a tortured groan.

RENEE PACED HER SMALL living room unable to sleep. She twisted her hands in agitation, not quite sure what she'd hoped would happen but definitely disappointed that nothing had.

Yet, the very fact that she'd looked into his eyes and felt a tingle zing from her stomach to her feminine parts made her extremely wary. She wasn't supposed to be attracted to John Murphy. The man had complicated her life in a way that should make him Public Enemy #1 in her eyes but she was slowly seeing him in a different light.

And that was not good. Better to keep the battle lines firmly drawn. They were not on the same side. They were simply being civil to one another for the sake of the kids. Kinda like being stuck in a loveless marriage…yeah…she knew what that felt like.

This year was not going to be Renee Dolling's year of living dangerously but rather the year of practical and sound decisions that do not encourage her to drink. Okay, so the thought wasn't something she could put on an inspirational button but it had to keep her on the straight and narrow. Thus far, it had. And that was saying something after all the stress and disappointment she'd endured while searching for her girls.

She sighed. Technically, she *could* date. She was past the prescribed time of no dating after making her commitment to sobriety but somehow keeping her distance seemed so much safer for everyone involved. No entanglements. No conflicts. No…sex.

That's where the pacing came in. Renee stopped and rubbed her palms down her jeans to wipe away the sudden clammy feeling. Sex. She missed it. Needed it. God, *craved* it.

But not with John Murphy.

Anyone but him. Why not, a voice whispered in her head and she nearly barked in laughter. Why? Because that man would likely brand her soul if he so much as touched her in a sexual manner. If they breached that intimate barrier there'd be nothing stopping her from falling headlong in love with him. Was that a bad thing? Yes! She didn't want to love John Murphy. She wanted to leave Emmett's Mill and put this whole awful chapter of her life behind her. She wanted to start a new life with the girls somewhere else. Was that so much to ask?

Her hormones seemed to think so because even as she berated herself for shooting periodic looks of intense longing toward John's house, she couldn't stop wondering what it might feel like to sample just one taste of that firm, sexy mouth.

Climbing into bed, she closed her eyes with an unhappy frown and tried to ignore the twisting tendril of achy tension that taunted her lady bits without mercy, reminding her that no matter how hard she may try, her curiosity was not fading but simply becoming stronger.

Well, she knew what curiosity did for the cat. She just needed to keep that reminder front and center in her mind when she started to feel her defenses drop around that man. That way her panties wouldn't drop, as well.

CHAPTER TEN

JOHN AWOKE EARLY AND, BEFORE anyone else on the ranch was up and around, made a trip to town.

Gladys needed a few things from the grocery store and the girls needed a laundry list of school supplies. But really, as he drove, it wasn't his list that preoccupied his thoughts.

It was Renee. Sleep didn't come easy and when he finally did succumb to a fitful state of drowsing, Renee filled his dreamscape in a variety of different states of undress. Really, that was plain ridiculous. He hadn't been so preoccupied with a woman since…well, it was in high school, he knew that much.

Needing a change in scenery, he went straight to the sheriff station to talk with Sheriff Casey about something that was gnawing at him more so than Renee.

Pushing open the double doors, he greeted Nancy with a nod. "The sheriff in?"

"She is. May I ask who…oh, wait a minute, you're John Murphy, aren't you?"

John nodded. "Guilty."

"How are those girls you inherited?"

"Doing good as to be expected I suspect, given their circumstances. Ranch life seems to agree with them, Taylor especially. She loves the horses."

"Bless their hearts," Nancy exclaimed then shook her head with a tsking motion. "It's so good of you to take them in with their mother being a fruit loop and all. With a temper no less."

"Renee's not a bad person. You just didn't see her at her best."

"I'm not saying anything to the contrary, but she did seem a bit unstable if you ask me."

John resisted the urge to comment further realizing that the receptionist was an avid gossiper and just looking for fresh fodder. Well, she'd have to get it elsewhere.

Nancy seemed to recognize her well of information had just dried up and buzzed him through to the other side. He went straight to Sheriff Casey's office.

Pauline Casey, a friend of John's since high school, smiled when she saw it was him.

"I see you made it past Nancy. What brings you into town? I know you hate to leave that ranch of yours. Oh, by the way, you worked a miracle with Tabasco. We were afraid we were going to have to put him down until you got your hands on him. Now he's a wonderful horse. You've earned that reputation of yours."

John didn't roll his eyes but wanted to. Somehow he'd been dubbed the Horse Whisperer of Mariposa County and he was pretty sure Evan had something to do with it. "Glad to hear he's doing better. Can I talk to you about something?"

Suddenly all business, Pauline nodded. "Sure. What's wrong? Something with the girls?"

"In a way. I've been thinking about the father. What happens if he shows up wanting to take the girls away? Can he do that?"

Pauline's stare hardened. "No way in hell that's going to happen. We have an I&B out for his arrest on charges of child neglect, and cruelty to a minor."

"What about the arsenic? Can't you slap him with attempted murder?"

"Hard to prove. A defense attorney could just say that Chloe, being as young as she is, could've accidentally ingested the stuff when he wasn't around."

"We have the girls' testimony that he made Chloe eat eggs that he made for her special. Isn't that enough?"

"I wish it were. Damn, I wish it were. Trust me, I want to get this guy as much as you but we have to have something that will stick or it will hurt the case against him, which could land those girls back in his custody on a technicality."

John felt himself pale but he managed to grit out, "Not on my life. Those girls aren't going anywhere near that bastard. He tried to *kill* Chloe. You and I both know it."

Pauline nodded. "I hear you, John, and believe you, but we have to do things the right way or else it could backfire and screw everything up. But before you get yourself all worked up, it's likely the girls would end up in protective custody before they'd land back in his hands, at least at first. You know family reintegration is a top priority if the parent can be rehabilitated."

His mouth curled in disgust. "The only thing that would rehab that son of a bitch is a bullet to the brain."

"Careful now," Pauline warned. "Talking like that can get you in trouble. But don't worry, they're not going anywhere just yet so let's cross that bridge when we come to it."

He supposed she was right but it made his gut curdle at the thought of letting that man even a hundred yards within the girls and damn, if that didn't make his trigger finger itchy.

Pauline deftly changed the subject. "How are things going with the mother? She any trouble?"

Distracted, he waved away Pauline's question. "She's not a problem. Not yet, anyway," he grumbled, his thoughts still sour.

"I'm surprised I haven't had a call from you saying she's tried to up and steal them in the middle of the night. She seemed the type to grab and run."

Pauline's offhand comment startled him. He'd never thought of that. Suddenly, he felt uneasy. Would she do that? He didn't know her at all and Alexis clearly didn't trust her. Perhaps he'd been too quick to let her move in. And what if he'd kissed her? What a royal idiot he was. She could be playing him for all he knew. It wasn't like she was trustworthy. She was an addict for crying out loud. She was probably a pro at lying to get what she wanted. He realized Pauline was watching him closely and he gave her a short nod as if in thanks. "I'll keep an eye on her," he said. "Who knows what she's capable of."

"Smart thinking."

Pauline seemed ready to play the amiable devil's advocate as she added, "Then again, she got off to a bad start here but maybe, deep down, she's a good person and if she's given half a chance, she could be a good mother again. Who knows. Stranger things have happened. Remember that time Fudder found that two-headed snake down by Hatcher Creek? Creepy little thing. The snake, not Fudder," she said with a small chuckle. "Anyway, hopefully things will work out for everyone involved. This is an unusual case."

Yeah, you could say that again.

Pauline offered a wise smile and John realized there was a wealth of unsaid knowledge behind that subtle twist of the lips. "What?" he asked, eyeing her suspiciously.

"Nothing."

"Nothing my ass. What's with that look you just gave me?"

She leaned forward, her gaze intent. "Have you considered what it's going to be like when your chicks fly the roost? Their mom is going to regain custody eventually."

"I know," he admitted with a slight scowl. "That's good. My life can get back to normal."

"True. But what if normal to you now is what you want normal to be forever?"

He balked initially at Pauline's question but once it sank further into his brain he realized she might have a point. When the girls went on with their lives…he'd miss them. A lot. He drew a deep breath and shook his head.

"We all adjust, right? No matter what the situation. That's life."

"True again," Pauline agreed.

He cleared his throat and focused on the one thing he felt he could control. "I want a restraining order against Jason Dolling."

"For your protection?"

"No, for his."

"I don't follow."

John met Pauline's curious stare. "If he comes on my property. I'm going to shoot first and ask questions later. He's not getting near the girls. I made them a promise and I aim to keep it."

"Consider it done. But John—"

"Yeah?"

"Don't shoot him. Just call us and we'll take care of things."

He tilted his head at her and offered a slow, dangerous smile, saying, "I'll call but no promises on what kind of condition he'll be in when you arrive. Drive fast. See you later, Pauline. Give Roy my best."

RENEE FINISHED PUTTING the dishes into the dishwasher and caught a glimpse of Alexis lurking around the corner. Pretending not to notice, Renee began to hum a tune she used to sing when Alexis was small.

Taylor and Chloe were in the rec room, attempting to play a game of pool, though neither could actually handle the pool sticks very well so they were just rolling the pool balls into the corner pockets on their own. Chloe was too short to really see much above the table so Taylor had to help her. Renee could hear their giggles from the kitchen and it warmed her heart.

"How's school so far?" she asked casually as she wiped down the tiled counter. "Do you like your teacher?"

"He's okay." Alexis slid around the corner but stayed close to the hallway as if she wanted to remain near an exit. "He has really big ears. Like an elephant."

"All the better to hear you with, I suppose," Renee said, holding back a smile.

"That's what he says, too."

"Sounds like he has a pretty good sense of humor about them."

Alexis shrugged. "I guess." She slid a little closer.

"Well, I hope no one is mean to him just because he's a little different."

"No. Everyone likes him so they don't call him names."

Renee folded her dish towel and hung it to dry on the oven handle. "What do *you* think of him?"

Alexis's expression was quietly reflective as she answered. "He's very nice. He doesn't make me feel behind even though I am."

Renee wanted to kiss this man. Or at the very least

shake his hand. "That's a wonderful trait in a teacher. What's his name?"

"Mr. Elliot."

"Nice name for a nice man. Taylor likes her teacher, too. Mrs. Higgenbotham. She calls her Mrs. H. for short."

"I would, too. That's a long name and it sounds made-up."

"I agree."

With the kitchen clean, there was little else busy work to do so she took a seat at the kitchen table and hoped Alexis would follow. She held her breath as Alexis seemed to consider the idea and then slowly slid into the chair opposite her.

"So, how long are you staying?" Alexis asked.

"I'm not going anywhere."

Alexis looked up sharply, her eyes lighting with wary hope. "You mean, you're going to stay here with us at the ranch...forever?"

Renee sucked in a breath and proceeded with caution. "Alexis...when the time comes and we get this court situation figured out, you, me and your sisters will leave the ranch and John can get back to his life."

Alexis stood up abruptly, her expression darkening. "I don't want to leave the ranch. Or Mr. John. If you want to leave, then go. But we're not going with you."

"Sweetheart, that's not possible," Renee said, trying to appeal to her sense of logic. "This is not our home—"

"It's not *your* home. Don't try to take us away from it."

"Alexis, wait…let's think this through a bit. What happens if—sometime in the future—Mr. John falls in love with someone? And he starts a family with this person? Where does that leave you girls? Just because we don't live with him any longer doesn't mean we can't be friends, though, right?"

Tears welled in Alexis's eyes but she didn't let them fall. Renee almost wished she would just so that Alexis would allow her to comfort her. But her daughter remained stoic and it really broke Renee's heart to watch.

"You should marry Mr. John then," Alexis announced as if that were the answer to everyone's problem.

"M-marry John?" Renee nearly choked on her own spit. She couldn't quite believe those words had tripped out of her daughter's mouth so easily. "That's not going to happen."

"Why not? You made a deal to take care of us and clean the house, what else does a wife do?"

Uh. "There's so much more involved, sweetheart. Things that a nine-year-old wouldn't understand."

"Like kissing?"

Renee nodded reluctantly and felt her cheeks redden. "Sort of. But kissing is definitely involved."

"Well, maybe you could work on the kissing part. And maybe you could get him to like you enough to marry you. Because we're not leaving."

And then Alexis turned on her heel and left the kitchen.

Marry John…good Lord. The thought was enough to curl her hair.

CHAPTER ELEVEN

SATURDAY, THE CRISP WINTER morning broke early and bright despite the forecasts of rain and snow, and John wasted little time in getting outside to get some things done.

His little shadow, Taylor, donned her alligator-green galoshes and her winter coat and promptly followed him out the door.

He glanced back at her. "Going somewhere?"

"We've got chores to do, right, Mr. John?"

He nodded. "Want to help me feed the horses today?"

"You betcha."

"You betcha? Where'd you learn that?"

"From Mrs. H. She's always saying it and I like the sound of it so I'm gonna say it, too."

"I see. Well, let's get to the stables. I can almost hear Vixen kicking the stall door wanting to know what's holding up the gravy train."

"Vixen is very big but not as big as Cisco," Taylor observed, falling into step with John. "Cisco is like a giant. But he doesn't scare me. He's sweet and he nibbles on my hand when I give him sugar cubes. I think it's sad that someone was mean to him. He's so pretty." She looked up at him, a wealth of trust and childish innocence shining in her hazel eyes, as she asked, "Why are people mean sometimes?"

He knew she was asking about more than cruelty to animals and he wished he knew the answer but, frankly, he didn't know why people did the things they did. "I don't know, honey. Sometimes people just aren't right in the head and they take out their frustrations on other people or their animals. They're bullies, plain and simple. But you know what? Bullies are really cowards because they only pick on those who they think won't or can't fight back."

After a long moment, Taylor nodded sagely. "I think my daddy was a bully. What do you think?"

"I think you're right."

She slipped her mittened hand into his and when she looked at him again, his heart contracted at the sadness and fear he read in her expression. "Mr. John, is it bad if I don't want to see my daddy again?"

"No."

"Good." Her relief was palpable. "Because I don't think I want to see him again ever. He was real mean to Chloe and he scared me. Sometimes when he looked at us, it's like he wished we were gone. You never look at us like that and I like it here. You're not ever gonna make us leave are you, Mr. John?"

"If it were within my power, honey, you could stay for as long as you want but your mama is here and she wants to rebuild your lives together. Don't you want that?"

Taylor nodded solemnly. "Yeah, but why can't we just all stay here? Renee has a nice little house in the back so she doesn't take up much room. Plus, she makes really good cookies, as good as Grammy Stemming, don't you think?"

"There's more to the situation at hand than good cookies," John said, wishing it were really that simple. If only all of the world's problems were easily solved by a warm batch of snickerdoodles. "But I'll tell you what, let's not worry about things we can't do anything about today and just enjoy the time we have together. How's that sound?"

"It sounds like a co-pro-mise."

"That's a big word and you're right again."

"Well, Mrs. H. is full of big words and she says that one a lot. She'll be happy to know I used it. She says our brain grows when we add a new word to our vo-cab-u-lary. Is that true?"

"If Mrs. H. says so, than it probably is." He chuckled and gave her hand a squeeze. "What say we get to our chores before Vixen tears down the entire barn?"

She grinned up at him, revealing the sweetest smile he'd ever seen, and he wondered how he was ever going to manage to say goodbye to three little girls who stole his heart the minute they showed up on his doorstep.

GLADYS FELT HER AGE TODAY and that was a hard thing to admit even if she was only admitting it in the privacy of her own thoughts. But this morning her bones felt as if they were grinding against one another and her arthritis finally kept her from working on her crochet project.

"You okay?"

Gladys startled at Renee's voice. For a moment, Gladys had forgotten she wasn't alone in the house. She stopped rubbing at her wrist and smothered the grimace for the younger woman's sake. If there was one thing Gladys hated, it was the pity of strangers. "Oh, just fine. Didn't hear you come in." She paused. "You're doing a good job, by the way," she added with a brief smile but the pain in her joints prevented a long-lasting effort.

"You come sit down," Renee instructed gently, yet the firm set of her mouth said she wouldn't take no for an answer. "There's nothing in the kitchen that needs to be done just this second."

Gladys waved her away with a slight frown. "Don't make a fuss. I've got a schedule to keep. It's Meatloaf Monday, you know, and if you start deviating from your schedule, the next thing you know you'll be eating spaghetti when you should be eating shepherd's pie. Puts your digestion in a tailspin. Plus, John loves Meatloaf Monday."

That last part was delivered in a wheeze that Gladys immediately found pitiful and if it hadn't rattled out of her and had come from someone else, Gladys would've told that person to stop being such a stubborn fool and take a load off. But Gladys was of the "Do as

I say, not as I do" generation and she wasn't of a mind to change her ways at this juncture of her life.

"I doubt your precious John Murphy is going to keel over dead from a digestion—what did you call it—*tailspin?* just because he didn't get his Meatloaf Monday. Now sit your rear in that chair and relax before you crumble to dust right before my eyes and I have to clean up the mess."

Gladys stared but a low snicker popped out of her mouth surprising them both. "I see where the girls get their spunk," she said and then in spite of her previous declaration shuffled to the wide, comfy chair directly in front of the fireplace and sank into it. She gestured at Renee impatiently. "So, come and keep me company then if you're going to make me sit here like the old lady that I am. There's no way in hell I'm going to sit on my duff while you do all the work around here. If I'm going to be lazy the least you can do is help me pass the time while I do it."

Renee smiled and after putting another log on the fire, sat on the sofa and tucked her legs up under her. "How long have you been making John meatloaf?"

"Since his mother died."

Her smile faded and Gladys was sad for that. She had a beautiful smile when she chose to show it. But Gladys appreciated her respect. Addie Murphy had been her best friend. Even after all these years, the pain of her passing hadn't completely faded. "When Addie died those boys were so lost, especially Evan, and John felt the pressure to keep everything together. This

Send For
2 FREE BOOKS
Today!

I accept your offer!

Please send me two free *Harlequin®* *Superromance®* novels and two mystery gifts (gifts worth about $10). I understand that these books are completely free— even the shipping and handling will be paid—and I am under no obligation to purchase anything, ever, as explained on the back of this card.

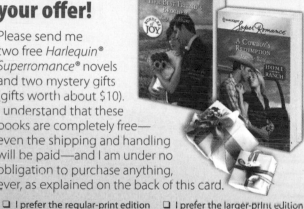

❏ I prefer the regular-print edition
336 HDL EYKF   135 HDL EYP3

❏ I prefer the larger-print edition
339 HDL EYKR   139 HDL EYQF

Please Print

FIRST NAME

LAST NAME

ADDRESS

APT.#   CITY

STATE/PROV.   ZIP/POSTAL CODE

Visit us online at
www.ReaderService.com

Offer limited to one per household and not valid to current subscribers of *Harlequin® Superromance®* books.

Your Privacy — Harlequin Books is committed to protecting your privacy. Our Privacy Policy is available online at www.eHarlequin.com or upon request from the Harlequin Reader Service. From time to time we make our list of customers available to reputable third parties who may have a product or service of interest to you. If you would prefer for us not to share your name and address, please check here ❏.

◄ Detach card and mail today. No stamp needed. ◄   H-SR-07/09

ranch was all they had, all Addie had after that dirty rat husband of hers turned tail and ran leaving them with a hill of debt and, well, meatloaf seemed the only comfort I could offer them."

Gladys happened to meet Renee's gaze at an opportune moment and caught a softening. It was probably not Renee's intention to allow that small slip and it caused Gladys to wonder. And because Gladys was known to dabble in business that was none of her concern, she decided to put her arthritis to good use.

"Maybe you're right. I don't think I'll be able to cook tonight. These old hands are cramping pretty bad. It's that darn storm that blew through here. Haven't been myself since. Rotten old bones." She leveled a finger at Renee and shook it at her playfully, saying, "Don't get old. It stinks. Can you believe this old body went white-water river rafting just a few years ago?"

Renee's eyes widened and Gladys chuckled, loving the shock value of the statement. "Yep. Went down the Colorado. It was Evan's suggestion and damn if I didn't shock everyone and go and do it." Gladys leaned in to whisper, "I think everyone half expected me to land in the drink but no, I did quite well. Had the time of my life. You should try it sometime. Evan can probably get you a discount."

Renee shuddered. "No thanks. I'm afraid of water. Now, tell me more about this Meatloaf Monday business. Is it hard to make? Maybe I could use the recipe and make it for you?"

Gladys smothered the triumphant grin. Young people nowadays were just too easy to figure out. She sent a silent prayer to Addie if she was listening or watching and asked for a little help in making things turn out right. Lord only knew it was time for John to settle down and why waste a perfectly good opportunity when it was staring everyone right in the face?

RENEE COULDN'T BELIEVE SHE WAS actually playing Betty Crocker but there was no denying that it was her mouth that had offered and it was her standing before a hot oven, worrying that John wouldn't like it or that she'd somehow messed up the recipe.

Well, it was meatloaf, she countered to the prattle in her head. How hard could it be? Mash up some meat, throw in some bread crumbs, a little egg and season. And then cook it to death. At least that was how she used to make meatloaf, but, come to think of it, she'd never won any awards for anything that came out of her oven.

So she was nervous. Understandably.

"Renee, that smells very good," Taylor said, taking a break from her coloring book to smile encouragingly at her mother. "It smells like Loafmeat Monday. How come Grammy Stemming didn't make it?"

"She wasn't feeling well," Renee answered, looking distractedly at Taylor, then added, "Honey, think you might want to call me Mom now?"

Taylor thought for a moment and then said, "I will take it under con-sid-err-ation. That's what Mrs. H. says when we ask for something in class."

"You're sure using lots of big words these days," Renee observed, smiling. "Imagine what you'll be saying after a full year of school. I might need a dictionary to keep up with you."

Taylor giggled and her eyes twinkled in a way that made Renee's heart sing. Suddenly Taylor looked quite serious, "So, Grammy Stemming makes smashed potatoes to go with the meat. Did she show you how to make those, too? 'Cuz we can't have the meat without the potatoes, that's what Mr. John says. He's a meat-and-potatoes kind of guy he says."

Taylor's statement dripped cute but the message Renee caught and processed in her brain just made her blush. John was all man, that was for sure. It was almost unfathomable that he was still single. Renee had to wonder what was wrong with him that some woman hadn't snatched him up long ago. She itched to know more about him but there was never a truly opportune way to nonchalantly dig for clues when the man rarely uttered more than a sentence or two. John Murphy wasn't what anyone could call verbose. She cleared her throat and smiled. "Of course. You can't have Meatloaf Monday without potatoes…that would be like cake without ice cream, or pizza without cheese."

Alexis piped in as she walked in from around the corner. "Or peanut butter without jelly."

Renee grinned, absurdly pleased that Alexis was playing along. "Right," she agreed. "So, the only question we need to answer is, red potato or russet?"

"Red, with the skins on," Alexis said. "I mean, that's how Grammy Stemming made them and they tasted pretty good."

"Sounds perfect."

Renee rummaged around for the potatoes and found them with a little help from Taylor who seemed to know her way around quite well and tried using the relatively mellow moment with her girls to start getting to know them again. The problem was, each time a question popped into her brain, she quickly discarded it for fear that it would come out wrong or Alexis might hightail it out of the room. She bit her lip. The silence grew and Renee started to feel the walls close in until Taylor began chirping as if she hadn't noticed the awkward moment.

"How come we don't have a grammy?"

"Excuse me?" Renee stammered, as the total off-hand delivery of the question caught her off guard. "What do you mean? You have a grandmother."

"Where?"

"Uh…" Renee stalled, suddenly wishing for a slice of that god-awful silence again, yet when she noted Alexis watching her keenly for a reaction, she cleared her throat and opted for a vague version of the truth. "Well, you've met your grandma Irene, uh, once I think, but you're probably too young to remember and as far as your dad's mother…oh, goodness, she died a while before you were born."

"Why isn't our grandma Irene around much? Doesn't she like us?"

Renee tried a disarming grin but her middle child's innocent question struck a sour chord and made Renee flinch. "Of course she does." That's a lie. A big fat one at that but she wasn't about to tell a child that her grandmother was as cold as a Michigan winter when it came to her only daughter and any of her issue. Renee remembered the phone call she'd placed when Alexis was born and how badly it had gone down. Just one more shitty memory she'd tried to erase with plenty of booze. She scrubbed her hands down the apron she'd found hanging in the broom closet and forced a smile. "So who's going to help me with these potatoes?"

Alexis's sharp gaze caught the fidgety movement and Renee had to fight the urge to shove her hands in her pockets to hide them. She smiled Alexis's way and tried to communicate without words that she'd changed. But the moment was lost. Alexis slid from the chair and scooped Chloe along with her. Renee longed to chase after her but Taylor was still beside her, chattering like a magpie, totally oblivious to the emotional tide that had just swept out, and Renee clung to her middle daughter's open nature as if her life depended on it because in a way…it did.

JOHN HADN'T EXPECTED RENEE to roll up her sleeves and hit the kitchen but he wasn't about to complain. One might think that after so many years of Meatloaf Monday a guy might get sick of it but he truly found comfort in the constant and it wasn't lost on him that Renee had tried to accommodate him.

The girls had cleared the dinner plates and Alexis was running the bath for her sisters. It was just him and Renee left in the room. He ought to say something nice. He ought to…stop his eyes from sinking to the midlevel of her fuzzy sweater and taking up residence. Glancing away, he absently tapped the table with his knuckles. Clearing his throat, he offered a gruff, "Dinner was good."

She looked up and gave a short smile. "Thanks." Then shrugged. "Taylor was a big help. She must love spending time with Gladys or something because that girl certainly knows her way around a kitchen. Not sure how I feel about that," she admitted with a slight frown.

"What's wrong with a girl being at home in the kitchen?"

"Because it gives men the wrong idea."

Wrong idea? His mother had been a whiz in the kitchen. That was a bad thing? "I'm not following you."

"Forget it."

"Tell me."

"I just don't want my girls to think all they're good for is to be stuck in the kitchen, you know? They're smart girls. They deserve better. I want them to go to college and make something of themselves."

"Did you go to college?"

"No." She looked away but not before John caught the stark look of regret in her stare. It pulled and poked at the soft side of his underbelly. He shifted in his

chair as if to escape but there was no relief. She continued, "Which is why I want better for my girls than
just being a housewife, stuck in the kitchen with a
passel of kids hanging off them."

He startled at the bleak and insulting view she'd just
shared of her opinion on what he'd considered the
greatest gift a woman could give to her children and
couldn't stop the stiff comment that followed. "My
mother was a housewife."

Guilt flashed in her expression and she lifted her
shoulder in apology. "I'm not putting down anyone
who chooses that life. I just don't want that for my
girls."

"And what if it makes them happy?"

"It wouldn't." Her answer was short and vehement.
She recovered with a subtle smile but her shoulders
were tense. If he wasn't so riled at her comment he
might be tempted to ease the knots out of the soft flesh
but as it was he wanted to tell her to get off her high
horse. And while she was at it, why didn't she pull out
the stick that was wedged up her rear.

"There's nothing wrong with a woman who wants
to spend time raising her kids right. But if you're the
kind of woman who would rather dump her kids off
at day care and forget about them for a good eight or
nine hours a day that's your own business, but don't
go judging others on their choices because they're different than yours. And your girls should be free to
make their own choices even if it doesn't cotton to
what you want them to do with their lives."

Her smile was wintry. "How nice of you to go all parental when you've never had any children of your own. Perhaps you'd like to write a book on the subject? I'm sure it'll be a bestseller."

What a sassy mouth on this one. All piss and vinegar as Gladys would say. He leaned back in the chair and regarded her with shrewd objectivity. "Your mom a career-type?"

"She was an image-is-everything type," she answered, probably unaware that she had visibly tensed. "Why do you ask?"

He shrugged. "Just wondering. Seems you're pretty sensitive about certain things. You and your mom don't get along?"

She barked a short laugh as if the question wasn't worth answering because the answer had to be patently obvious but the sound was ragged and tattered around the edges to John's ears. "Must be my lucky day. First Taylor, now you. Is this some kind of conspiracy to get me to work through my feelings about my mom? Look, I'm over it. To answer your question, no, me and the mom don't get along so well. In fact, I'm pretty sure if I was on fire she wouldn't waste a drop of spit to put it out."

He whistled low and deep. That was pretty hard-core. John understood that kind of animosity. It was about the same way he felt about his own father. "What happened between you two?"

"It doesn't matter. It was so long ago I'm not even sure I remember."

"I think you remember just fine."

She shot him a dark look. "Maybe I do. Too bad for you, I don't feel like walking down memory lane."

"Fair enough."

"Really. Just like that. First you're grilling me and now you're fine with letting it go?"

He shrugged. "Sure. You don't want to talk about it. It doesn't interest me enough to coax it out of you."

"Aren't you a charmer," she said drily and he chuckled in spite of the vague insult she'd just thrown his way but he couldn't dispute it. He was no good at this talking shit. The woman didn't want to talk about why she was so sensitive about her mom, it was none of his business.

"That's me. Grade A Choice."

He got up, ready to leave the faintly aggressive tension between them behind, but she cocked her head to the side and regarded him as if he were suddenly someone who fascinated her.

"Why don't you wear a cowboy hat?"

He paused and returned the assessing stare as he countered, "Why don't you like housewives?"

"I asked you first."

He shrugged. "I'm not a cowboy. I just work with horses. There's a difference." He pinned her with a look. "Your turn."

She inhaled sharply and for a split second he was sure she was going to turn tail and run but she didn't. Instead she answered with an unwavering but undeniably sad stare.

"Because I never wanted to be one but somehow that's where I ended up."

CHAPTER TWELVE

RENEE SLID INTO BED AND WINCED as the cold blankets shocked her skin. She'd left a fire burning in her small woodstove but sometimes the heat didn't make it to the tiny bedroom and it felt like she was sleeping on a block of ice until her own body heat started to kick in.

What an odd man, she mused as scenes from dinner replayed in her head. He was an enigma. Just when she thought she knew what he was about, he went and turned her assumptions upside down, leaving her to gape in confusion. She sensed something between them. Something that ran hot one minute and cold the next. Wasn't that a bad thing? If she were made of glass such rapid change in temperature would surely cause her to shatter. Well, thank her lucky stars she wasn't made of glass, she thought wryly. One thing was for sure, he was frightfully good at reading people. Or maybe he was just good at reading her. Now *that* was a scary thought.

What had she been thinking? Meatloaf Monday. How ridiculous. She should've left him to fend for himself. Damn, if she hadn't always had a soft spot for the weak and vulnerable. Um, yeah. Who was she trying to call weak and vulnerable? Certainly not John Murphy. Cornbread farm boys with wicked smiles did not grow up to be weak or vulnerable. They grew up to be men who filled doorways, with thick roping muscles honed from years of working with their hands, and quick, sharp gazes that saw through piles of bullshit to the truth underneath.

Gazes that lingered and caressed the tingling flesh under your sweater until your nipples peaked and ached and all but poked out of your bra for need of someone to put their big strong hands all over them.

She shuddered and moaned as she gave her pillow a sound whack for even allowing her mind to wander into such dangerous pastures—uh, territory!—even her metaphors were going country. Good grief. Was it contagious?

Rolling to her stomach, she tried quieting her mind with deep breathing exercises and for a while it worked. Slowly her mind emptied of everything involving John and his big, strong man-hands and what she wanted him to do with them, and she focused on the calm, serene landscape of her favorite place—a picture of a waterfall in Maui, a place she'd never been but the image always soothed her—and slowly drifted into peaceful slumber.

She wasn't sure why her eyelids fluttered open; the darkness told her sunrise was still hours away, but seconds later she caught the faint but undeniable sound of a child screaming inside the house.

Kicking herself free from the tangle of blankets, she ran shoeless and fumbling in the dark, toward the sound, mindless of the rocks that bruised her heels and the bitter cold that froze her exposed skin. All that mattered was getting to her children.

ALEXIS HELD CHLOE CLOSE, rocking her in spite of her sister's frantic attempts to get away from the invisible hands that tried to hurt her. Alexis's heart felt ready to jump out of her chest as tears filled her eyes but she didn't let go. She just kept murmuring in a soft, soothing voice that everything was okay and that no one was going to get her.

Taylor huddled against the headboard, her thumb popped in her mouth like she always did when she was scared, scrambled from the bed and catapulted herself into John's arms the minute he appeared in the doorway, eyes bleary but searching for the cause of Chloe's fear.

Renee nearly crashed into him as she pounded down the hallway.

"What's going on?" she asked, breathless, moving toward the bed until Alexis shook her head vehemently. Hurt crossed her mother's features but she stopped. "What's wrong with Chloe?"

"She gets nightmares sometimes," Alexis answered, pulling Chloe closer even as the baby shook and shivered. "I can take care of her. You can go back to bed."

Taylor wrapped her arms around John's neck all the

more tightly. Her voice watery and frightened. "It's Daddy's fault, Mr. John. It's all his fault Chloe is so scared at night."

Renee looked at Taylor, confusion and fear crossing her features. For a moment, Alexis was tempted to let Renee take over just so Renee could feel Chloe shake in her arms but instead her fingers tightened around her little sister and hoped they'd all just go away. "Just go back to bed. I'll handle it."

Renee turned to John and murmured something and he nodded reluctantly, taking Taylor with him. Renee approached the bed. Alexis scowled. "I said, you can go."

Renee shook her head and took a seat beside them. Alexis felt tears stinging her eyes and tightened her grip on Chloe. "I can do it," she insisted. "I've been the one here for her. Not you."

"I know," Renee acknowledged quietly. "What do we do to help Chloe?"

Surprised to be asked, Alexis answered haltingly, "She's not awake when she does this and if you try to wake her up too fast she just starts screaming and kicking. I just hold her real tight and tell her it's okay. She seems to like that."

Renee nodded, tears filling her eyes. "How long has this been happening?"

"Since Daddy started locking her in the closet with the spiders and the other bugs."

"Your daddy…he did that?" she asked, her voice breaking.

"That's not all," Alexis said. "He—"

"I understand," Renee cut in, her eyes filling again.

"No, you don't," Alexis whispered, anger seeping inside her, hot and mean. Chloe whimpered and she loosened her hold until Chloe's breathing returned to normal. "Because if you did...you never would've left us behind. Especially Chloe."

And then the tears she swore she'd never let her mother see, started to pour out of her eyes in a way she couldn't control and it made her all the more angry. "Please get out. We don't need you."

"Alexis—"

"Get *out*," she cried and her mother drew back. The hurt in her expression giving Alexis no joy even though she'd thought it would. She choked on her next words. "Just leave. *Please*."

RENEE FORCED HER FEET TO MOVE. This was not the time to press the issue although she yearned to take her baby in her arms and cuddle her as she should. She paused at the doorway and saw Alexis settle into the bed with Chloe lying against her small chest, her fingers clutching Alexis's forearm.

Swallowing a toxic mixture of grief, fear and guilt that had congealed in her throat, she started to return to the guesthouse when she saw John talking with Taylor in a low voice in the living room. Not wanting to be seen, Renee pulled into the shadows and listened intently.

"My daddy is a bad man, isn't he?" Taylor asked,

the sadness in her tone cracking Renee's heart for the sorrow in it. "Why was he so mean? Are we bad girls?"

"Of course not," John answered softly. "Why would you say that?"

Taylor hiccupped. "Because maybe if we were better, Daddy wouldn't have been so mad and Renee wouldn't have left. And then, maybe Daddy wouldn't have been so mean to Chloe. Chloe's not a bad girl, even if Daddy said she was. I don't believe him and neither does Alexis. Do you think Renee thinks Chloe is bad? Sometimes she pees the bed but she doesn't mean to. She just forgets and has an accident. You would never spank Chloe for having an accident, would you?"

"No, I wouldn't and I don't think your mom would, either."

"You don't?"

There was a long pause and then he answered solemnly, "No, I don't."

His answer pierced Renee's chest in an unexpected manner. She wasn't accustomed to others being in her corner, much less a man who made it no secret of how he'd felt about her from the very beginning.

Renee melted against the shadows, wishing she could dissolve into a spray of mist and just disappear so that she could escape the awful feeling crushing her. Tears stung her eyes. *What the hell did you do to our babies, Jason?* He only hurt *your* baby, a voice whispered. Chloe was no blood relation to him but he'd been raising her as his own. For all intents and purposes, Chloe looked at Jason as her daddy. And yet, he'd done unspeakable things to her. In essence, she'd left her baby in the hands of a monster. Biting her lip hard to keep it from trembling, she slipped out the back door unnoticed.

THE NEXT MORNING, JOHN ROSE and went about his chores with Taylor beside him. Last night's excitement all but forgotten, she chattered amiably to the horses as she gave them each a good scoopful of oats while he busied himself with throwing out the hay and filling the giant buckets with fresh water for the day. While Taylor may have been fresh-eyed, John's mind was haunted by the stricken expression frozen on Renee's face after Alexis had tossed her out of the room. He'd been tempted to help smooth things over but his hands had been full with Taylor and he figured Alexis and Renee had to start working things out on their own. To his mind, that wasn't going too well. For too long Alexis had been acting like a surrogate mom and didn't know how to let go of the reins, so to speak, and Renee, too riddled with guilt and whatnot, couldn't just pull forward and assert her authority.

It was a pickle—one he shouldn't give a whole hill of beans about, either, but damn if he wasn't getting a headache over the predicament.

"You about done over there, half pint?" he called out to Taylor and she nodded, running over to return the oat pail to its peg on the wall before skipping to his side. "Did you double check the gate latches?" he asked.

"Yep. Have you figured out how you're gonna get Vixen to stop stomping on your helpers?" she asked, an excited gleam in her eye. "Yesterday, I thought she was going to stomp Mr. Tony to death! She was so mad that he was trying to come into her stall."

"Yes, she was. And, no, I haven't figured that one out yet. She's the toughest horse I've ever worked with."

"Someone was mean to her, huh?" Taylor asked, her eyes solemn. "That's why she don't like no one. What happens if she *never* likes no one? Will you keep her forever here at the ranch?"

He shook his head. "She doesn't actually belong to me, half pint," John said, his mouth twisting sadly. "Her owner is paying me to gentle her so that he can ride her."

"I don't think Vixen would like that very much," Taylor said, shaking her head like a miniature version of himself. He would've laughed except the subject matter was rather serious. Vixen's fate was dire if he couldn't get her on the right track. Her owner wasn't known for his compassion. He'd bought Vixen because she was beautiful with solid lines and a proud disposition but he hadn't listened when the seller had tried to tell him that she wasn't no kiddie pony. Now, she was so riled and cantankerous, if John couldn't get her under control, she was bound for the glue factory. And that was a crying shame, one that he tried not to think about. Returning his attention to Taylor he ruffled her blond mop, chuckling as he said, "Is that so? Well, we'll do our best with Vixen. Until then, it's school for you. Run on and go see if your sister is awake yet."

"Yessir, Mr. John!" Taylor saluted John with a lopsided grin and took off running for the house, her blond hair fluttering behind her like a kite tail, tugging a grin from his lips before he could stop it. If he'd ever seen fit to settle down and raise a family he knew he would've wanted a daughter just like that kid. He couldn't imagine walking away from his kids, not even if his life depended on it.

RENEE PEEKED IN ON GLADYS, anxious for something to do, and was surprised when she saw the old gal up and moving around.

"Aren't you supposed to be in bed?" she asked, a frown creasing her forehead. "You look pale."

"Takes more than a fever and some sore bones to keep me down. Besides, I promised Chloe chocolate chip cookies and there's no sense in lying down when there's stuff to be done. Right?"

"I suppose," Renee said, feeling worlds from this stout old lady. Back when she and Jason were still married they used to spend whole days doing nothing except making beer runs. The house had been a pigsty, beer cans overflowing the small plastic garbage can, and pizza boxes littering the kitchen because neither one of them could do much more than speed dial with any efficiency. Out of nowhere her cheeks started to burn for her own laziness. She'd been raised differently and so had Jason for that matter but it hadn't mattered. They'd both acted slovenly.

"Something on your mind?" Gladys inquired when she noted Renee had stopped folding the blanket in her hand and it was hanging limp from her fingertips. Gladys gestured and Renee snapped to attention with a flustered apology but Gladys waved it away. "No need. You know, I think we ought to get to know each other better. Seems you're not the person I might've thought you were."

Renee startled. "What do you mean?"

Gladys shrugged, making no excuses. "My opinion of you was pretty low until recently. I know it's not right but the first time I met you I thought to myself, 'Now there's a flighty, snooty slip of a girl' and then of course, if you were shacking up with Jason you couldn't be worth all that much because frankly, that boy was never going to amount to much, bless my sister's heart for never giving up on him." Renee stared, unsure if she should be offended or not but Gladys didn't seem to mind and kept talking. "I suspect you two have been living off the inheritance my sister left for you when she died?"

There was no sense in denying it. The money—not that thirty-five thousand dollars was a lot in the big scheme of things—had allowed them to party un-checked, unhindered by jobs or other inconsequential things, and gloss over the major problems in their marriage. The burn in her cheeks flared bright as she nodded and her throat seemed to choke off her voice.

"We were going to buy a house," she said. "But it never worked out."

Gladys continued to tidy the room but the ensuing silence made Renee wish she'd bypassed the old woman's room. "We made a lot of mistakes," she admitted after a long moment. Gladys glanced up and seemed to nod in agreement. "But I'm trying not to live in the past. If I keep looking backward I'll go crazy. It's bad enough that I can hardly get near Chloe because Alexis blames me for everything that happened after I left, and the guilt and shame is enough to kill me already. I don't need to overload myself with the stupid mistakes Jason and I made with his inheritance. I feel bad enough."

"You know…I believe you."

Renee met Gladys's steady gaze and felt tears well in her eyes but she wasn't willing to trust so simple a declaration. How could Gladys feel anything but disgust for her when she'd clearly been a terrible mother to her three children, abandoning them with a man who was not fit to raise a dog? "Is that so?" she said, unable to keep the mocking tone from her voice. "And why is that? I seem to recall you saying that you didn't think much of me when we first met."

"True enough. But I've seen the heartbreak in your eyes over what your girls have been through and I don't believe you ever meant to hurt them or put them in harm's way. I know Jason didn't start out a good-for-nothing. It was a process of evolution. I blame the drugs."

"Oh…" Renee whispered, cringing that Gladys knew. "How'd you…"

"A person doesn't blow through the kind of money you two were blowing without a little help. He called me a few times looking for money. I turned him down. I knew it wasn't going to help things. I told him to get a job and earn an honest wage. He hung up on me. That was the last time I heard from him until the night he dropped off the girls. I hardly recognized him. He'd always been on the thin side but he looked no more than skin and bones. A ghost in ripped and faded jeans with hollowed out eyes. You don't get like that unless you're doing something terrible to your body." Then Gladys pinned her with a hard look. "The question is…were you doing drugs, too, Renee?"

It was an honest question and Renee tried hard not to bristle but it was difficult to allow another person to poke around in your personal business without getting at least a little defensive. She swallowed hard before answering. "No. I never did that…but I am…an alcoholic, which is no better…no worse."

"You go to meetings?" Gladys asked.

"Yes. Every Tuesday evening, even when I was on the road. I'd grab a local newspaper, the listings are usually in the community events section. Although, to be honest, I don't attend the Emmett's Mill meetings. I've been going to Coldwater."

"Afraid people are going to judge you." It was a statement, not a question. "Smart. It's hard to make a fresh start with everyone knowing when you've fallen and skinned your knee."

Renee nodded, grateful for the woman's under-standing, though why she cared, she hadn't a clue. She suspected it had something to do with her ragged emotional state but it was a relief not to have to be on guard for the moment. "I do want a fresh start," Renee said, unshed tears filling her eyes. "I just don't know how to go about it."

Gladys chuckled and patted her arm. "Well, I believe I can help in that department. But first, we bake. Chloe is getting her chocolate chip cookies today because a promise is a promise. Don't you agree?"

Renee thought of the string of broken promises she'd left behind in a trail of failures throughout her life but in her mind she heard Chloe's terrified shrieks and it gave her strength. She gave a resolute nod. "Yes," she said, making the answer a solemn vow inside her heart. *No more broken promises...*

LATER THAT DAY, AS JOHN WAS picking up Alexis from school, he was thankful Taylor was released at noon rather than at the same time as Alexis. He needed to have a private talk with Alexis, but he wasn't quite sure how to broach a certain subject. He ought to just leave well enough alone and let Renee sort out her own mess with her daughter but the fact was, he wasn't doing it for Renee.

Alexis was hurting, even if she didn't want anyone to know. Clearing his throat, he rested his hand atop the steering wheel and drove at a slow clip as if he had all the time in the world when in fact he had more to do at the ranch than he possibly knew how to accommodate within a twenty-four-hour period. Mentally assigning a few extra jobs to the "helpers" as Taylor liked to call them, he drew a deep breath to begin but Alexis must've sensed something for she launched enthusiastically into her day. John wasn't fooled. Alexis was never this chatty.

"And so this girl, I don't really know her name, she likes this guy, I don't really know his name, either, and they kept passing notes back and forth all day and it was so *annoying*. Now that I'm back in school, I can't really remember why I wanted to return. I mean, all the kids care about are stupid things like iPods and cell phones and who has the coolest clothes…it's all so dumb and *juvenile*."

"Juvenile?" He couldn't stop the chuckle that followed. "That's a pretty sophisticated word for a nine-year-old."

She leveled a stern look his way that nearly broke his heart for its misplaced maturity and said, "Please. Now *you're* just being dumb. I may be nine but I can't remember the last time I worried about anything so…" She searched for the right words and came up frustrated. Seems as much as she might like it otherwise, her vocabulary was still on the limited side. "Well, I don't know…stupid."

He sighed. Alexis turned to glower out the window and watch the scenery pass them by. He was tempted to just let the silence continue but he knew that wasn't the prudent thing to do, especially when they were dealing with such a sensitive subject. "I need your help, Alexis," he started, risking a quick glance her way to gauge her reaction. He wasn't disappointed, her head tilted subtly indicating she was listening. "I think Chloe and Taylor could benefit from talking to someone—you know like a counselor who specializes in traumatized children—after everything they've been through. What do you think about that?"

At the mention of her sisters she went into protective mode. It took a long moment before she answered. "I don't know…maybe it might be good. Especially for Chloe," she admitted.

"That's what I was thinking. But you know it might be good for you, too."

She looked at him sharply, her fine-boned features narrowing in suspicion. "Why me? There's nothing wrong with me. I don't need to talk to anyone."

"That's where our opinions differ. You're pretty mad at your mom. I think it might help to talk to someone about it."

She snorted. "How's that supposed to help? Is this her idea? Did she put you up to this?"

He shook his head solemnly. "No. The blame falls squarely on my shoulders."

Alexis turned away, her gaze finding the scenery again. "Well, I don't want to. Taylor and Chloe can go. I don't need it. Just send Renee away and everything will be fine. I can take care of my sisters and you. We don't need her, anyway. I can't believe I actually told her she should marry you." She laughed, but that sound coming out of her small mouth was harsh and unforgiving, and John had his answer even if it wasn't something she was going to agree with. "She should just leave. Everyone would be happier."

"You think so?" he asked, though he knew the opposite to be true simply by the sad quiver in her stiff upper lip. "Well, we'll have to see what happens. In the meantime, I think you ought to consider what I said."

She shot him a dark glare but remained quiet. Something told him her silence wasn't voluntary. He had a feeling if she'd tried to say anything the tremble in her voice would reveal far more than she was comfortable sharing.

He knew that anger, how it mixed with fear and longing to jumble a young mind. As often as he'd gone to bed every night hating his father for leaving like the coward he was, there were times when he was ashamed to admit he would've done anything to be relieved of the burden he carried for his mom and brother. He rubbed his chin absently. He'd been a teenager when their dad flew the coop. It was a lifetime ago but he remembered the anger…the same anger he felt radiating from the little girl across the seat from him. But there was something else he remembered and this part was probably the same thing that was tripping Alexis up, too—as much as he'd hated his father, a part of him had still loved him. Just like Alexis loved her mother. No matter how hard she tried not to.

RENEE WENT VERY STILL. "You think my girls need…
professional help?" *Badmotherbadmotherbadmother*—
the damning words were all she heard in her head no
matter how she tried to remain calm and rational. Her
shoulders tensed but she tried a disarming smile as she
continued to clean the kitchen after that night's dinner.
"Well, maybe when we get settled somewhere else I'll
look into it," she offered with a shrug. "But for now…I
think we all have our hands full with just getting
through this weird custody…uh, situation."

"You won't." His knowing comment almost made
her drop the bowl in her hand. Carefully placing it on
the counter, she turned to face him. His tanned face,
creased at the corners of his eyes from too much time
spent in the sun, scanned her own and she felt ridiculously exposed. The man saw too much and that was
dangerous.

He continued softly, "You're just saying what you
think I want to hear."

"So? What difference does it make? My girls are
not your concern. I appreciate your suggestion but I
don't agree with you. All my girls need is to get out
of here and back to a normal life."

He stood abruptly. "A normal life? Is that what they
had with you?"

God, no, but she wasn't going to admit to that. It was
going to be different this time around. She lifted her
chin. "I'm their family. Not you. I decide what they
need. And what they need is something less…uncer-
tain."

He expelled a short, annoyed breath. "All you know is uncertainty. If you don't know what it's like to be stable how are you supposed to give it to the girls? What's your plan if you get custody back? What then? Just pack them in the car, close your eyes and let your finger drop on a map?"

"And what if I did?" She shot back, hating that he'd struck a raw, very tender nerve. She didn't know where they would go but at least they'd be together and that's what counted, right? She threw the dish towel to the counter and closed the distance between them. "And what do you mean *if* I get custody back? It's a matter of time before the judge comes to his senses and I get my girls."

"You're not going to drag those girls around while you try to figure out what to be when you grow up. They have stability here. And you're ignoring a very serious issue because of your own damn insecurities."

She gasped and took a faltering step backward, her eyes stinging as surely as if he'd backhanded her. "How dare—"

With the quick movement of a rattler striking, he jerked her to him, his grasp rough but his eyes held a tender caress that stopped the breath in her chest. "Woman, stop thinking of only yourself. Those girls need you to be their mama…not their friend or buddy. And they *need* professional help." He held her tightly, his mouth compressed to a hard line but her stomach twisted in confusion when her own lips parted as if in invitation. He pulled away slowly. "They need their mama to do what's right for them. Even if it doesn't feel good and damn near breaks your heart to do it."

The tears that sprang to her eyes a second ago slipped down her cheeks and she swallowed convulsively. "What if the counselor makes them hate me even more? I left them. What kind of mother am I?" Self-loathing curdled in her stomach and her mouth suddenly hungered for the smooth, liquid anesthetic of a shot of Jack Daniel's. For a split second, she could nearly taste it at the back of her throat. Horrified, she sprang from John's arms and immediately put a good distance between them. "I can't."

"Can't what?"

Can't feel anything for you. Can't let anyone else into my girls' heads. Can't forgive myself for leaving them in that situation. Oh, God…can't *deal*…

"Renee?" John's soft voice pierced her heart clean through and she took a step back as he took one forward. "Wait…"

She put her hands up, stopping him with a whisper. "No." Shaking her head, she backed away. She had to get away from him, from the feeling in her chest, from the ache in her heart. It was too much.

CHAPTER THIRTEEN

OVER THE NEXT FEW DAYS John and Renee kept their distance from one another, both preferring to keep what had happened between them locked in the privacy of their memories. They made polite, stilted conversation for the girls' sake until John felt ready to jump out of his skin.

Sitting across from her at the dinner table, Gladys seated to his left while the girls filled the rest of the empty seats around them, John wondered if this was what hell felt like.

Gladys tucked into her lasagna with gusto, proving that something as small as surgery couldn't put a damper on her appetite, and John pretended not to notice the furtive glances Renee sent his way when she thought he wasn't paying attention. What a right mess he'd made of things, he groused silently, shoveling a large bite into his mouth before he was tempted to let the words percolating in his brain fly. He didn't know much about recovery or the process or even what it entailed aside from avoiding whatever it was that put you in that situation in the first place, but he did know that Renee was acting like a fool about this counselor business. Now was no time to start acting selfish but that's exactly what she was doing.

"John? Did you hear me?" Gladys broke into his turbulent thoughts. She frowned. "You're as friendly as a winter bear right now. What's got you all twisted up tonight?"

He shot an accusatory glare Renee's way but his gaze slid away before Gladys could call him on it. He shook his head and stuffed another bite in his mouth, speaking around the cheese burning his tongue, "Nothing. Just hungry."

Gladys eyed him speculatively but let it go for Taylor, as usual, filled the silence with her chatter until she'd exhausted all her pent-up news for the day. Chloe giggled as Taylor slumped against her chair with a melodramatic sigh and declared, "Yep. Mrs. H. says learnin' is hard work and it must be true 'cuz I'm exhaus-ted. May I be excused, Mr. John?" She let loose a yawn and rubbed her bleary eyes. "I think I better hit the haysack."

"It's hit the hay, dumb-dumb," Alexis muttered, earning a frown from Renee that she completely ignored as John nodded. "C'mon, I'll get your bath ready."

Chloe and Taylor slid from their chairs ready to follow their sister when Renee stood and intervened. "I'll get their baths ready, Alexis. You go ahead and finish your homework."

"I'll do it after their baths."

Renee placed her napkin down with a gentle, restrained movement that mirrored the subtle pull of her lips as she tried asserting her authority again. "No. I want to help the girls. Go on. Please don't argue with me."

Alexis looked to John or Gladys for help and when neither seemed ready to back her up, she lifted her chin and threw a "whatever" over her shoulder before disappearing from the room in an angry huff.

"Preteens," Gladys quipped as if teenage hormones were to blame for Alexis's attitude. She helped herself to another garlic bread as she said cheerfully, "Well, look at the bright side, you only have seven more years before she returns to normal. Not so bad if you ask me. Although I never had kids of my own so who am I to judge?"

Gladys chuckled at her statement and took a big bite.

"Maybe you ought to go easy on the bread and butter, Gladys," John said, more than a little alarmed at the way Gladys was eating without regard to her doctor's orders. "You trying to clog another artery?"

"You hush. I don't tell you how to eat now do I?"

"I didn't have a triple bypass," he commented wryly, watching as Renee put her plate away and walked from the room with the little girls' hands tucked into her own. She wore a smile but John sensed the pain it was hiding. The situation with Alexis was killing her but she was too damn stubborn to ask for help. Even from a professional.

As soon as Renee was out of earshot Gladys dropped the innocent chatter and pinned John with a look that made him squirm in spite of the fact that he was a grown adult.

"What's going on with you two?"

"Nothing."

"That's a line of bullshit if I ever heard one. I may be old but I'm not blind. There's definitely something going on and I want to know what it is."

He stood and took his and Gladys's plate to the sink even as she protested that she wasn't finished. He arched one brow at her. "I'm not going to watch you put yourself into an early grave with a second helping of lasagna."

"Fine. But you're not going to stop me from having a cookie. Bring me one, if you please."

He sighed and selected the smallest on the plate. Handing it to her, he leaned against the counter. "I think Renee and the girls should see a counselor," he admitted slowly, looking up to catch Gladys's reaction. Hell, maybe Renee was right and he ought to leave well enough alone between them but as Gladys, a woman he trusted above all others nodded her head in understanding, he felt a weight drop from his shoulders. "What happened to them…it's left its mark. I think it's more than Renee can handle."

"Perhaps."

Wait a minute… "What do you mean *perhaps?* I thought you agreed with me."

"Johnny-boy, you always were a smart one but you

have a lot to learn about how a woman thinks, especially a mother."

"What makes you say that?" He tried not to be offended but his ego felt a little tweaked.

Gladys smoothed the crumbs from the surface of the oak table into her palm and rose to deposit them into the trash. "You can't possibly imagine the guilt that woman is feeling about what her girls went through. From the outside looking in it's easy to assume that she's being selfish for not wanting to send her girls to a shrink. But think of things from her side of the door. Would you want someone to know your private hurts and humiliations and be judged for them?"

"It's not about her." He wanted to snap but somehow kept his voice calm. "It's about the girls. They need help."

"I don't disagree with you. But she's not ready to take that step with them and it'll have to be together or they'll just get in each other's way. She needs to believe that she's a good mother before she can let someone else come in and start poking the tender spots. You understand?"

"Sort of," he admitted. "So what should I do? I can't just sit by and watch as Chloe continues to scream at night and Taylor is terrified that her daddy is going to show up and take them away and Alexis…she's so angry. I don't want her to grow up with that inside her. It can warp your mind."

Gladys's warm gaze told him she understood that he

spoke of something he knew well and she loved him for his sacrifice. "I don't want that for her," he finished quietly.

"I know. But you can't make Renee be the person you want her to be unless she's ready to go there herself. Give her time. She's scared and trying desperately to make things right. Just help her get there."

He didn't know how to do something halfway. Either he was in or he was out. And he knew there was no kidding himself that he was starting to think of Renee in more ways than just the mother of Gladys's wards. He was starting to think of the girls as more than just temporary roommates. And a part of him hated it. His life had been turned upside and inside out that rainy night and he didn't know how to make it right again. A sinking feeling in his gut told him that making it right had nothing to do with emptying his house of his guests.

And he was man enough to admit that scared the shit out of him. He was a bachelor for a reason. He was surly, cantankerous, a plain grouch on the best of days. Animals were the only ones who didn't seem to hold any of those traits against him.

Yeah, but let's be honest, when was the last time you felt satisfied with just a one-way conversation held in the barn with a horse's hoof between your palms?

It's been awhile, he admitted to himself and bit back the sigh that wanted to follow. That put him in a bit of a predicament that he didn't know the answer to but he knew it had *Renee* written all over it.

RENEE TUCKED HER YOUNGEST daughters into bed, trying not to let Alexis's attitude douse the joy that giving the girls their bath had created. Such a simple thing but God, she'd missed it. Singing "Oh, I wish I were a little bar of soap" with the girls as they giggled and splashed, washing their beautiful blond hair and then gently combing out the snarls gave her a peace she hadn't felt in a long time. Except for the fact that Alexis refused to look at her and when she did spear a glance her way, it was black with open resentment. Renee couldn't help but shrink away from that stark emotion, hating the echo of John's words in her memory.

She needs a counselor. So do you.

He was wrong. Her girls didn't need a head doctor. Just time to see that she'd changed. She risked a warm smile Alexis's way and was instantly rebuffed as Alexis turned, giving Renee her back.

"Alexis…" she whispered. "I love you."

In return, Renee received silence. She swallowed and vowed not to give up.

ALEXIS SAT ACROSS FROM the woman at the table and nerves made her tummy ache. The woman was from social services. She smiled a lot and scribbled notes on her little pad but Alexis knew things were not going well. At least not by Alexis's way of thinking. Renee was winning. At this rate, she'd have them packed up and gone within the hour if this kept up and Alexis was not going anywhere with her mother.

"Alexis, how are you enjoying your new school?" she asked.

"I love it," she answered eagerly, putting as much emphasis on the words as possible. Shooting Renee a dark look she added, "It's a better school than any of the schools I've ever been to."

"Oh? Have you been in a lot of schools?" she asked.

Alexis nodded. "Oh, yes. My parents didn't like to stick around one place too long. I guess right about when the bill collectors started calling is when we'd split. Isn't that right, Renee?" She looked innocently at her mother who was gaping at her in shock. Take that and choke on it, she thought smugly.

Renee colored and took a moment to clear her throat before defending herself. "We made a few mistakes here and there but I'm so glad Alexis has finally found a school she enjoys. That's all that matters."

Ms. Thin As A Pencil scribbled something down and Alexis desperately wanted to read what she'd written. Hopefully, it was something along the lines of "Terrible mother. Give permanent custody to John Murphy." But Alexis was pretty sure that wasn't going to happen without a little nudging, which she was plenty happy to provide.

"Do you always call your mother by her name?"

Renee jumped in before Alexis could answer. "Only recently. Things have been a little bumpy between us but we're working on it, aren't we, sweetheart? Before all this happened we were very close, Lexie and I. She was my little helper."

Alexis ignored Renee and gave Ms. Social Services a sad nod. "Well, someone had to pick up the booze bottles in the morning and get the babies breakfast 'cuz she and Daddy sure as heck weren't going to do it. Remember that time you slept all day and Chloe got a really bad diaper rash 'cuz you let her sit in a poopy diaper all day? I would've changed her but we were out of diapers."

Renee paled and her mouth compressed to a fine, tight line, so much so that Alexis wasn't quite sure if she was going to be able to get the words out but she did. Barely.

"Alexis, that's enough. Ms. Nagle doesn't want to hear about things that happened in the past. She wants to hear about how well we're all doing *now.*"

"You're right. Things are so much better now that Daddy is gone and you're no longer our mother." She turned to Ms. Nagle who was watching the scene unfold with alarm and pleaded with the woman. "Don't give us back to her. She doesn't want us. She just doesn't want Mr. John to have us because she's jealous that we're finally happy and she's not. I hate her and if you send us back I will run away and no one will never find me! I promise!"

Alexis spun on her heel and ran from the room, her heart slamming against her chest like something out of a cartoon as she burst from the house and headed for the open field behind the house. She ran until her leg muscles burned and her lungs felt ready to cave in. It wasn't until she'd collapsed in a heap on the cold ground that she realized it wasn't the wind stinging her cheeks but her tears. Folding in on herself, she cried until she had nothing left and her heart hurt and her guts felt sick.

She didn't want to leave.

RENEE STARED AT THE PAPERWORK that had come in the mail and tried to comprehend what she was reading. She looked up and thrust the paper in John's hands. "Did you have something to do with this?" she demanded, although a part of her knew he didn't but she needed someone to blame. He shook his head and for what it was worth, he seemed apologetic.

"No, I didn't but—"

"But of course you agree because it was your original idea in the first place," she said bitterly. "You win. Court ordered therapy for Alexis and myself to deal with—" she snatched the paper from John's hands "—Alexis's issues with her mother. It is my recommendation that the Dolling children remain in temporary custody of Gladys Stemming until the successful completion of six weeks of therapy. Further evaluation to follow." She slapped the paper against her thigh. "Six weeks!"

"First of all, calm down," John instructed, but Renee wasn't in the mood to listen to anyone, least of all him. "You're making a mountain—"

"Don't say it," Renee warned, her voice ending in an unattractive hiss. "Just don't. This is my life they're playing with. Not yours. No one is suggesting they root around in your head now are they?"

"What are you so afraid of?"

"Afraid?" she scoffed, yet her insides quivered. Everything! *I'm afraid that they'll find that Alexis is right. That I'm a terrible mother who doesn't deserve three beautiful girls.* She sniffed back a sudden wash of tears and swallowed the wail that was building on a wall of hysteria. "I'm not afraid of *anything.*"

"Good. Then you have nothing to lose by complying with the court's recommendation." He crossed his arms over his powerful chest and for a heartbeat Renee wished she could just fold herself into that solid warmth but she was fairly spitting at him in her misplaced anger and she doubted he'd welcome the attempt. Which, she realized, was better for the both of them.

"Glad to see you've come to your senses," he said, though they both knew he was mocking her because she was being irrational.

"Shut up," she said.

"Grow up."

Renee skewered him with a glower, which he matched. And then they both stalked from the room. In opposite directions.

CHAPTER FOURTEEN

RENEE PERCHED GINGERLY on the edge of the soft sofa designed to make her feel comfortable and fought the very real urge to bolt. Everything about the room made her uneasy, from the bucolic Thomas Kinkade prints on the neutral, taupe colored walls to the annoyingly distracting gurgle of the large water fountain in the corner. It was like having Niagara Falls in the corner of the room. Renee had never understood someone's desire to have fountains large enough to—

"You don't want to be here."

Renee cut her a short look. Brilliant observation, Doc. What tipped you off? Renee forced a short smile. "I'm fine. I just didn't realize I should've brought a life vest," she muttered.

The doc gestured toward the fountain. "Does it bother you? I can turn it off. Most of my clients find it soothing."

"It's loud."

The woman chuckled and clicked a remote control sitting on the delicate, antique table beside her. Silence filled the room. "Better?"

Not really. *Better would be listening to Bob Seger on the CD player as I blast out of this place.* Renee shrugged. "Fine. Let's get this party started."

The slender woman sitting across from her in a sumptuous leather chair that probably cost more than Renee's entire wardrobe sighed softly as she shifted position and smiled warmly. "All right then. You're here because the court believes you and your daughter could benefit from having someone to talk to."

Renee bit her tongue to refrain from saying something caustic and instead nodded her head.

"Well, first, I'd like to say I am not your enemy. I'm here to help. Your body language says you're holding in a lot of anger. Let's see if we can't identify the source and help to dispel it so you don't have to drag it around anymore." The brunette doctor gestured, adding with another smile, "So settle in and get comfortable. You're here for an hour. Might as well get the county's money's worth."

Renee sat back but the tension in her shoulders remained. The only kind of sharing she did was at her AA meetings and only because everyone there was going through the same issues. There was no judgment. Here—her gaze raked the professional woman seated across from her, watching from behind delicate yet devastatingly stylish designer rims—the doctor would certainly judge her once she heard the facts. And frankly, Renee wasn't interested in listening to one more know-it-all tell her what a bad person she was. She already knew. "Listen, Dr...." she took a quick look at the nameplate on the desk to the right "…Phillips—"

"Please call me Lauren," she broke in with another soft, doe-eyed expression that immediately set Renee's teeth on edge for its sweetness. The last thing Renee needed was to feel some kind of false security with this woman.

"Dr. Phillips," Renee repeated with a little frost just to get her point across. "Let's cut the crap. As far as I'm concerned you *are* the enemy. Maybe that's not fair but frankly, I don't care. Because of some dingbat woman who clearly could not tell that my daughter was playing a manipulative little game to get her way, I'm another six weeks away from getting my kids and getting the hell out of this place. And by *place* I mean both your professionally decorated office and this stupid, little town where they make up the rules as they go along, and people pay for legal services with a barter system, and it snows like a mother, and you have to keep a fire going 24-7 if you don't want to wake up with frostbite!"

Dr. Phillips, smile fixed to her lips as if it came with her outfit, scribbled some notes, prompting Renee to ask, "What'd you just write?"

The woman just chuckled and despite the soft nature of the sound, Renee got the distinct impression she'd just screwed herself again. When Dr. Phillips answered with a sigh, "I think we're going to need more than six weeks," Renee let loose with a juicy curse word that she rarely used but damn, it felt good to say it.

"All right then. Let's begin, shall we? Tell me about your childhood…"

Oh, goody. A trip down memory lane. My favorite.

Renee closed her eyes and wished the earth would swallow her whole.

JOHN DIDN'T HIDE HIS OPINION of the man standing before him, but he did bite back the names he wanted to call him since he knew Taylor was watching the whole scene from the stables.

"You've had her for nigh three weeks. What's the holdup? Aren't you supposed to be the best? That seems plenty time to break one stubborn horse."

John shifted his position just in time to avoid the disgusting splatter from Cutter Buford as he let loose a dirty stream of chewing tobacco juice.

"I told you, that isn't an ordinary horse. She's high-spirited and smarter than you. You knew that when you bought her. I'm making progress but I can't make any promises that she's going to be the horse you want her to be just because you're paying me to gentle her. The fact is, she might always be squirrely." John refrained from adding that Cutter's own mishandling of the horse had created a whole slew of new problems. Because of Cutter, Vixen didn't trust or *like* anyone. He'd only just gotten to the point where she didn't try and stomp him to death when he entered the arena with her.

"Shit," Cutter muttered, kicking at the hard, frozen dirt with the heel of his expensive, shiny boots. John held back a snort. Cutter was the worst kind of owner. Plenty of money to waste but not a lick of sense in his fool head to go with it. Cutter—if that was even his name. Rumor had it his real name was Ralph—was new to the area but was trying to build a reputation as a horseman. He *thought* he knew horses. Sort of like the city boys who came to the country to buy a ranchette and considered themselves cowboys because they owned a spotted cattle dog, a horse and a few head of steer. You can buy a tractor but it don't mean you know how to drive it just because you hold the keys in your hand.

Cutter cleaned the wad from his cheek with the stub of his finger and flicked it to the ground. When he spoke again, there were black flecks stuck in the crevices of his teeth that made John want to puke. "I'll give you two more weeks. Then, I'm taking my horse."

John nodded, but he wanted to stick his foot so far up Cutter's ass he could see the tops of his well-worn boots tickling the man's tonsils so he didn't trust opening his mouth. Thankfully, Cutter didn't seem to notice or care that John was a man of little words. He was already returning to his monster diesel truck, pausing only a minute to curse at the splash of mud dirtying the shiny chrome on the wheel well. John smirked. That ain't no working truck. Just as Cutter wasn't no horseman.

He felt a small hand curl into his own. He looked down and saw Taylor watching Cutter leave with the same look of contempt on her young face as he felt in his heart and it warmed him to the bone in spite of the cold. "I don't like him," she stated firmly.

"Me neither."

"Why can't we just keep Vixen?"

John glanced down at Taylor and his heart contracted at the simple question. Funny, it's about the same as he was starting to feel about the girls. Why couldn't he just keep them? All of them? A voice whispered, knowing he was thinking about Renee. He was attracted to her, that was for certain. Each night he went to bed with an ache in his groin and his mind full of things that shouldn't be there but the woman was enough to age him prematurely. Stubborn, mean-tempered, beautiful and dangerous. Hell...Vixen and Renee...sounded about the same right about now. And, yeah, he wanted to keep them both.

Too bad, neither belonged to him.

RENEE RETURNED FROM HER therapy session and from running errands to find the girls and Gladys gone. She wandered the house and still finding no one, she reluctantly sought out John to learn where the girls were. She found him brushing down that monster horse of his, talking low and soft as he did the job.

He was a handsome man, she'd give him that. Usually, cowboy types didn't do much for her, even though John said he wasn't one. To her untrained eye he looked the part, especially when he was handling that horse with such loving care. His hands, large and callused, made slow and easy progress down the horse's flank. She imagined when he put his mind to

something he didn't rest until he did it well. Her imagination obligingly provided a scenario of his hands
touching her in such a reverent manner and the tension
from the day lessened, though she would've thought
being in such close proximity would've been less than
soothing. But even as she watched him, a part of her
began to fill with languid warmth as tendrils of longing
curled around her senses and tightened uncomfortably. Of all the men in the world…why him?

He finished and with a final pat on the horse's neck,
he exited the roomy stall and startled at seeing her
standing in the doorway. "How long you been there?"

"Not long," she lied. "Where is everyone?"

"Gladys took the girls over to her place for a spell
after school. Said she needed to make sure her plants
weren't all dead. They'll be back before supper."

"Oh. Okay." Alone in the house. Ridiculous temp-
tation started to jabber indecent suggestions in her
head that frankly, made her wonder if she were
suddenly channeling a nymphomaniac.

"How'd your first therapy session go?" he asked,
effectively dousing the fire licking her insides as
easily as a bucket of water killed a campfire. Noting
her sudden scowl, he chuckled. "That good, huh?
Why am I not surprised?"

A grudging smile found its way to her lips in spite
of her decision to return to the house and she said, "Her
name's Lauren Phillips. Know her?"

"Nope. Contrary to what you may think, I don't
know everyone in Emmett's Mill."

"Just the important people. Like the sheriff. And the judge. And nearly everyone else I've come into contact with since landing in this place."

"True enough. So, what did you think of her?"

"I think she's an impeccable dresser with questionable interior design tastes," Renee quipped.

"I mean what did you think of her as a therapist?" John asked with only a hint of exasperation. "Do you think you'll feel comfortable talking with her?"

Renee leveled her gaze at him. "I don't think I'd be comfortable talking with *anyone* about my past. She could be Mother Teresa and I'd still want to run for the hills. Scratch that. I'm already in the hills. Stuck in the hills is more like it, actually," she muttered darkly.

"You don't like it here, do you?"

"What's not to like?" she shot back sarcastically. When he didn't retort, she softened only a little, saying with a shrug, "Well, it's not my first choice. I prefer places with a little less—" small-town prejudice, nosy neighbors "—snow."

"You like to live where it's hot all the time?"

"Remember? I came from Arizona. That should answer your question."

"Originally?" he asked, curiosity lighting his eyes in an inviting manner that she tried to ignore.

"Uh, why do you want to know?"

He shrugged. "No reason."

She supposed there was no harm in sharing that bit of information. "Yeah. Born and raised near Tucson."

"So you do like it hot."

She laughed. "I guess so."

"Well, if you stick around you'll see it can get pretty hot around here, too, come summer. And it's a dry heat, like your Arizona." He winked at her and she startled at the playful gesture. John wasn't the type to wink. But, as her smile grew, she realized she kind of liked the lighter side of John Murphy. Made her wonder just how many facets this man hid behind that tough exterior.

Also made her wonder if she had the guts to find out.

His cell phone rang at his hip and he answered it on the first ring. Listening for a moment, he pulled the phone away from his ear to ask, "You mind if Gladys and the girls go for ice cream?"

Renee shivered. "It's not quite cold enough already for them?" He shrugged as if he didn't know if that was a rhetorical question and she sighed before answering. "I guess that's fine. So much for dinner if they're eating ice cream so late in the day."

John returned to the phone. "That's fine just be careful out there, once the sun goes down the roads are going to slick up. A storm's coming." A moment later he disconnected and returned the phone to his hip.

Renee's ears pricked up as she glanced fearfully at the sky. "What kind of storm? A big one?"

"Sounds like a pretty good one. But don't worry, they'll be back before it starts."

Renee hated the idea of waiting out another storm all alone in that little cottage while everyone else was warm and snuggled together in the main house. "I wish Gladys would've told me she was in the mood for ice cream. I could've just picked up a quart of something while I was in town," she said, worried about Gladys and the girls on the road when the weather was about to get ugly. "I mean, honestly, for an older woman, she's not very bright. What if she gets into an accident with the girls?"

John chuckled and she jerked around to stare frostily at him. "You find this funny?"

"A little. Everything will be fine. You get yourself worked up about the oddest things."

"Is that so?"

"Yes."

"Well, I'm glad to hear you find me amusing."

The smile left his lips but an intensity returned to his eyes that immediately set her previous fire to smoldering again. She inhaled sharply, mildly alarmed at how quickly he could kindle desire with only a look her way.

"We should get back to the house," she said, licking her lips unintentionally yet her toes curled inside her boots as his gaze tracked the movement of her tongue. Blatant hunger shone in his eyes and caused her lungs to constrict in the most annoyingly female way that was at once delicious and telling. She wanted him, too.

He slowly stalked toward her and she backed away until her backside met the smooth wood of the stable wall and she could go no farther. "Wh-what are you doing?" she asked, trying for calm when in fact she felt ready to jump out of her skin.

John leaned in, one hand bracing himself near her left ear and he shocked her by taking a deep whiff near the soft, exposed skin of her neck. "You smell good," he said softly, his breath tickling her ear. "You know that?"

"Thanks," she whispered, unable to say much more without betraying the tremble in her voice. "You smell like horses," she managed to add, eliciting a low, throaty chuckle on his part. What she didn't say was that she didn't mind.

She risked a smile and looked into his eyes. Such soulful, deep and arresting eyes, she noted as she allowed her gaze to travel the lines of his face. "Why didn't some woman snatch you up a long time ago?" she wondered, realizing a half second too late she'd said it out loud.

"Never found the right one," John answered without hesitation. "I guess you could say I'm particular."

She uttered a short, soft laugh. "Then what are you doing here pressed up against me?"

"The one thing I swore I wouldn't do," he answered with a faint grimace but before she could react he took her mouth with his own, the offended retort dying on her tongue as she was suddenly busy with other things.

JOHN PULLED RENEE INTO his arms, his senses alive with the solid feel of her body against his, and gave into the tremendous wave of pleasure that came from the seductive dance of their tongues twining and retreating. It was a slow and steady assault on his defenses and it was a battle he didn't mind losing in the least. His groin tightened until his jeans bit uncomfortably into his taut skin and he wanted nothing more than to lay Renee down in the hay and warm every inch of that beautiful skin of hers. But even as desire attempted to blot out every useful thought in his head, there was a voice—faint as it were—demanding that he stop. For one, he doubted Renee would much enjoy a quick roll in the barn. She made it abundantly clear she was no country girl. And two, well, this just smacked of a bad idea on multiple levels.

But damn...for something so wrong, it felt pretty right.

Biting back a sigh of frustration, he pulled slowly away. Her lips, swollen and reddened, called to him and he had to catch himself before he leaned in for another taste. "I'm sorry..." he started, but then stopped. "I take that back. I'm not sorry. I've been wanting to do that for a while now and well...you looked so beautiful standing there that I didn't want to hold back. I am sorry if it complicates things more than they already are."

It was a moment before she spoke and the silence had started to make John sweat. Finally, she nodded. "I'm not going to lie. I'm attracted to you in the worst way. I want you so bad my teeth ache. But...what happens afterward? We may be playing house for the moment but eventually I'm leaving and I'm taking my girls with me. And then what? Broken hearts all around? No. It's bad enough that my girls are going to bawl their eyes out when we have to leave. Someone has to stay strong for their sakes."

"You're right," he murmured, regretfully putting more space between them. "It's a good thing one of us is thinking clearly. Because right about now I've got some crazy thoughts running through my head and I can't say they're not motivated by the wrong things."

She blushed a pretty shade of pink and he grinned. "Damn, you're beautiful," he said.

"Stop that," she said, trying to be serious, though her eyes had warmed with a sweet light. "How am I supposed to stay strong when you're handing out compliments like candy? I'm just as vulnerable as the next girl when it comes to sweet-talking men."

"Somehow I doubt that," he said. Moving toward the barn entrance, he jerked his head, saying, "Let's get out of this cold barn before we freeze and see what we can throw together to eat. If I can't feed one appetite, I can certainly feed the other, right?"

"Lucky for you, Gladys left a potato casserole in the oven. That woman spoils you rotten."

"It's true," John acknowledged with only a hint of cheeky laughter in his voice. "But if Evan were around she'd do the same for him. She's always been our surrogate mom since our own mom died," he said.

"I know. She told me. That woman thinks a lot of you two. You're really lucky."

He grinned again. "I know that, too. Why do you think she pretty much has the run of anything I own? It's because I know I could never repay her for what she's given to Evan and me. You can't put a price on that."

"No. You can't," she agreed softly and the wistful expression on her face made him wonder what her childhood had been like. Something told him it wasn't full of hugs and kisses and cozy Christmas mornings. His mother may not have had much in the way of money, but she always had an abundance of love and when she died, Gladys stepped in without a beat. A long, pregnant silence passed between them until John, not interested in ending the moment in melancholy, reached out and tugged gently on her hand.

"C'mon, I'm starved and it's not getting any warmer in this barn."

She returned his smile and he pretended not to notice the subtle sad pull at the corners of her lips as she allowed her hand to rest in his as they trudged back to the house. He let go first because he sensed it was coming. He tried to push from his head the urge to ask what was behind that enigmatic expression because he knew that was a boundary she hadn't invited him to cross. Hell, she'd pretty much just drawn the line in the sand and it was up to him to respect it. And he did. Fully. Even if knowing that he couldn't touch her in the way he desired was tying him up in knots.

But worse still than the knowledge that he couldn't bury himself in that soft and yielding body was the fact that no matter what happened between them, Renee couldn't get out of this place fast enough.

And that killed him.

He wanted her to stay. *Damn it*. He wanted her to stay.

Rubbing his chin at the realization, a dry chuckle followed. Well, if that didn't wedge him in a difficult spot he didn't know what did. But something told him he was about to get a helluvan education with Renee around.

CHAPTER FIFTEEN

RENEE STARED IN DISMAY at the fat flakes spiraling down from the slate-colored skies to land silently on the ground, and offered a nice, mean curse to Mother Nature for her winter bounty.

No fair, she wanted to grouse. It had snowed last weekend, too. Not a lot and not as much as the weatherman had predicted but it had prevented her from taking the girls on an outing. She'd shelved her plans for the following weekend, yet here she sat, muttering at the sky for ruining her plans—again.

"I hate the country," she said under her breath as she shoved another log inside the woodstove. "When I get out of here, I'm never going to live in another place where there's even a chance of snow. It's cold and you have to stay bundled up all the time and…and…" She searched for another reason to hate winter in the country but she was suddenly distracted by the undeniably sweet sound of her daughters' laughter out in the yard.

Dusting the bits of bark from her palms, she rose and peered out her small window to see Alexis, Taylor and Chloe twirling in the snow to catch flakes on their tiny, outstretched tongues. Chloe, unsteady on her feet, was the first to tumble to the soft snow. Taylor's unabashed joy shone in her young face as she fell backward without fear into a thick snowdrift. But even as her younger daughters made her smile with their giggles, it was Alexis with John that made her breath stop. She and John were building a snowman. It was lumpy and odd-looking but the smile wreathing Alexis's face brought tears to Renee's eyes just for the lost beauty of it. How long had it been since Alexis smiled at her like that? The lump in Renee's throat was answer enough. Her first impulse was to rush out there to be a part of their fun. But the fact that she hadn't been invited stung more than her pride. And so she didn't follow her instinct. Instead, she contented herself with leaning against the window and watching silently.

As she stood there, chuckling softly at their antics as snowman building turned into snowball wars, she realized how much her daughters had missed in their previous life. Jason had never spent so much time with their girls. For that matter, she hadn't, either. Her own mother hadn't been much for setting a motherly example, not that Renee was trying to use that as an excuse but it was true. Had her life with Jason always been an exercise in bad parenting? Every moment of it? She searched her memory, desperately seeking for something that wasn't coated in a haze of alcohol but came up empty. Her gaze returned to John and a sigh escaped her. She'd give anything to see Alexis turn that beaming smile her way. A tear surprised her as it snaked its way down her cheek. As she wiped it away she knew she'd do anything to deserve her daughter's love.

Pulling away, Renee let the lacy curtain fall from her fingertips, but was surprised by a soft knock at the door.

Opening it, her heart leapt as Taylor stood there.

"What is it, honey?" she asked, afraid to hope.

Taylor pushed her hair from her eyes and said breathlessly, "Grammy Stemmy and us are gonna make snow-cream. You wanna come help us?"

Snow-cream? She didn't have a clue what that entailed but since she was being invited, Renee didn't much care and her smile reflected as much. "Absolutely," Renee answered enthusiastically, wasting little time in grabbing her jacket and following Taylor into the yard where Gladys was instructing the girls in how to collect the snow.

Renee stopped. "You mean, you use the snow? The *actual* snow that's falling out of the sky? Is that safe? I mean, healthy?"

Gladys and John shared a look that plainly said "city girl" and Renee set her jaw in annoyance. "What?"

Once everyone had their large bowls full with fresh powder, they tromped back to the house, the girls' chatter filling the silent, white landscape as surely as it filled Renee's heart and for a small window in time she actually didn't hate snow any longer.

FIRE CRACKLING IN THE fireplace, it was warm where Renee was sitting but she wasn't sure if the heat came from the cozy fire or the hormones percolating her blood.

"Girls asleep?" she asked unnecessarily when John returned from one last tour of the house, knowing that he would've checked on the girls and Gladys along the way. He gave a short nod and then settled on the floor beside her. "Nothing wears them out faster than a day spent outside in this kind of weather," she noted, trying to keep calm and detached even though her heart had started to race.

"You've never had snow-cream before, have you." It was a rhetorical question. Her baffled expression had surely said it all as Gladys had poured an odd assortment of stuff in a giant bowl then whipped it together to create something that—bless her heart—was damn good.

"Not a lot of snow where I come from, remember?" she murmured, glancing at him from beneath her lashes. A small smile followed when he chuckled.

"You don't know what you've been missing," he joked.

"Apparently."

He nudged her gently. "C'mon, admit it. You thought it was pretty good."

"Yeah. It was. Although, I'm still not sure it's healthy to eat what's falling out of the sky."

"It's fine," he assured her and his easy smile was infectious. He lifted a stray strand of hair away from her cheekbone and tucked it behind her ear. The action was enough to steal her breath. For what it was worth, it seemed she wasn't the only one affected. "I'm going to have to kiss you," he said softly.

"Oh?" She tried to seem disinterested but it was a losing battle that she gave up on real quick. Her tongue darted out to lick her lips and she knew it would seem like an invitation. He wouldn't be wrong. He leaned in and sampled her lips, moving slowly and sensuously across the surface of her mouth, tongues touching, exploring and stroking in such a way that Renee lost her ability to recall why she'd put a stop to this type of behavior in the first place. At that particular moment Renee would've pointed a gun at anyone who caused him to stop.

They kissed as if there was no rush. The moment was all about exploration and John used the same single-minded attention he used with his work on her body. His hands searched and roamed every hill and valley until Renee felt as if he'd memorized every inch and it made her feel valued and cherished in a way she'd never imagined possible. She hardly noticed when her clothes fell away, but the moment he peeled his own clothes off, she sucked in a wild breath as her gaze traveled the hard, toned and muscular body of a man accustomed to making a living by the sweat of his brow. His hands were rough and calloused and they excited her in a way she'd never known. Jason's touch had been soft and impatient as he grabbed and pinched for his own pleasure, regardless of what she liked or wanted, but she'd stopped trying to get him to be more considerate long ago. She sucked back a gasp as John kneaded the firm flesh of her breast, teasing the nipple through the fabric of her bra and any residual memory of Jason or any other lover faded from her mind.

They might've remained there if not for an errant sound outside that reminded them they were in danger of being discovered by any one of the houseguests and neither relished the idea of being caught in an indecent position. So with her hand tucked into his, Renee grabbed her clothes and followed John into his bedroom and closed the door softly but firmly behind them.

MOONLIGHT REFLECTING OFF the white landscape outside dusted the room with pale light and danced on Renee's naked skin, giving it a luminance that seemed unworldly. John's heart beat an erratic rhythm that labored his breathing as if he'd just spent the afternoon splitting wood with a dull-bladed axe. He'd never seen a woman so beautiful. Her eyes shone with vulnerability mixed with desire and it made his vision swim with the power of it.

Bracing himself above her, one heavy thigh trapped between the soft, silken skin of her legs, he leaned down and kissed her deeply, pausing only long enough to make sure she wanted this as much as he did.

"I wouldn't be here if I didn't," she assured him in a husky whisper. "I want this. I want you."

Her words thrilled him unlike any other and he claimed her lips again but he was hungry for the rest of her and his appetite was no longer whetted by just the taste of her lips. Pressing an ardent trail of kisses down the column of her soft neck, her sharp intake of breath encouraged him to go farther, until he reached her full breasts. Lavishing each one in turn with his mouth, he didn't rest until she was twisting and writhing beneath him, clutching at his shoulders and begging him for more.

Sliding down farther and ignoring the near painful ache in his groin as his hard length demanded to know her fully, he took her into his mouth with slow and measured strokes taking quick note of which strokes elicited the best response and as her thighs started to shake with gathering need and she began grabbing the bedsheets in her clenched hands, he brought her home with loving attention.

RENEE EXPLODED, GASPING as she climaxed harder than she ever thought her body capable. *Heaven help her, the man had talent!* Head lolling to the side, trying to draw breath into her lungs, she barely had time to form a coherent thought before John was drawing her pliant and sated body to his. His tongue swept her mouth, the smell of her own musk igniting the fire once again, kindling the banked desire as if it had not been just satisfied.

His eyes gleamed with a dark and sexy light that told her he was not nearly finished with her and she wasn't wrong.

Flipping her to her stomach, he rained kisses down

her back, hitting erogenous spots she hadn't been aware existed, and as he drew her to her knees her arousal hit a plateau that made her wild with need. She'd never been fond of this position, always too conscious of how her behind might look but at this moment, she felt incredibly sexy and wanton and when John seated himself to the hilt the last thing on her mind was if he was thinking she could stand to lose a few pounds.

His strokes took on a tell-tale urgency and his labored breathing gave Renee a dark, powerful thrill knowing that he was nearing his release. That coupled with the hard glide into her body, hitting the deepest most elusive spot inside her, sent her hurtling toward her own release that shocked and delighted her as she'd never been able to reach the Big O from sex alone. She tensed as he did and they tipped over the edge together, collapsing to the bed, panting with the force of what they'd achieved with near perfect synchronicity.

It was several moments before either spoke but as the sweat dried on their bodies, Renee was relieved to see that a condom wrapper was on the floor. She hadn't realized he'd even put one on but she was ridiculously grateful that at least one of them had been thinking clearly enough to use one.

Renee turned away so that John could discreetly dispose of the used condom but in doing so, the moment seemed to turn awkward. She got up to retrieve her clothing but John's hand gently pulling her back to the bed stopped her.

"I should get back to my...um, house, cottage-thing," she whispered, not quite sure what to call the small guesthouse. "I don't want the girls to see me come out of your room in the morning."

"It's a long ways before morning," he reminded her and her gaze sought the alarm clock beside the bed. It was several hours before dawn. The entire house was still sleeping soundly. Was he interested in Round Two? His lips lifted in a smile but there was nothing suggestive about it. "Stay a bit longer," he said, drawing her into the shelter of his arms without waiting for her response. As John nuzzled her neck she tried not to think how wonderful it felt to be snuggled against him but her body betrayed her.

"I can't stay long," she finally said, settling against him, telling herself it was only for a few more minutes longer. "The girls..."

"I know," he said, the faint hint of resignation in his voice telling her he understood but his arms tightened around her just the same. Her eyelids drooped against her will. It was too comforting, too inviting to remain there in his arms. For something that smacked of a terrible idea, it sure felt good.

Was it the phenomenal sex, she wondered silently. It had to be. Who knew John Murphy was a love guru? She tried to look past what had happened between them because it was too real, too big to acknowledge but it stared at her with the unwavering gaze of a predator stalking its prey. It was just her style to fall in love with a man whom she had no business fooling around with.

It was *so* her style. Self-destructive, stupid and selfish. Yep. That was her style all right. So much for changing patterns.

"Stop."

She startled, all traces of sleep gone from his voice. She turned to face him, his expression, illuminated by the silvery light streaming from the frosted window-pane, was troubled and knowing. It was the knowing part that made her want to run. "Stop what?" she asked.

"Stop thinking whatever's running through your head," he said.

"What makes you think I'm thinking about any-thing?" she tried bluffing but he saw through her and that made him dangerous.

"You've got that look on your face," he said, smoothing her forehead. "A subtle frown that says you're upset about something."

"What's to be upset about? We're two consenting adults. We didn't do anything wrong. Everyone needs release every now and again." She watched him from beneath her lashes, holding her breath against the reaction she knew her words would cause.

"Release. I see," he said, moving away from her. "That's all it was to you?"

"Wasn't it for you?"

"Yeah. Sure." His answer was flippant but his sharp movements as he jerked his boxers back on told a dif-ferent story. She winced inwardly because deep down she knew she was hurting him even if he was too prideful to let it show. But, really, who were they kidding? It wasn't as if she was going to move in and be his little country wife and he was going to adopt three kids that weren't even his. In what kind of world does that happen? She lived in the real world even when it sucked.

She made quick work of finding her clothes and putting them back on, all the while avoiding any eye contact with John. She didn't want to see the pain that would be there. Didn't want to acknowledge the odd ache in her own chest that rightly shouldn't be there. Get real, Renee! You don't fall in love with a man after only two months of knowing him. She paused at the door and met his gaze briefly. "Let's keep this between us, okay? I don't want the girls to know," she said, not expecting the cold look he sent her way.

"I've already forgotten about it," he answered and her knees threatened to buckle from the wave of hurt that followed but she'd be damned before she let him see it.

She stiffened. "Great. So have I."

Taking care not to slam the door behind her when in fact she wanted to bring the house down with the force of her pain, she gritted her teeth against the cold and made the short, slippery walk back to her little cottage. Each step affirming her decision that playing house with John Murphy had been the stupidest idea on the planet.

CHAPTER SIXTEEN

RENEE STARED MOROSELY at the expensive off-white Berber carpet covering the expanse of her therapist's office and wished she had control over the passage of time. If she did she'd zip past her mandatory meetings with Dr. Perfectly Put-Together and move straight to the part where she received the all clear to get the hell out of this place.

"Tell me what's bothering you today," Dr. Phillips suggested, her unwavering gaze soft and knowing at the same time, and Renee shifted in her chair. "The last few sessions have gone so well, yet today it seems… you've had a setback. What happened?"

I think I fell in love with a man who's totally inappropriate for my life. As usual. Obviously, this therapy stuff wasn't working. She speared the doc with an annoyed glare. "Can't we just skip to the part where you tell social services that everything is fine and I deserve to get my girls back?"

Dr. Phillips smiled her answer, which clearly said Renee was asking for the moon, and merely waited for Renee to open up. Surprisingly, and almost against her own will, Renee started talking, or rather, her mouth just started blurting out things that under ordinary circumstances she would never share. Either way, the cat was out of the bag.

"I slept with John Murphy. And it was good. No, it was better than good. It was mind-blowing and frankly, I didn't even believe that sex could reach that kind of level but it did and it's messing with my mind. I mean, *really* messing with my mind because now I've been wanting things that are impossible and ridiculous—"

"Such as?"

Renee scowled at the doctor. "Such as things that are completely out of my reach."

Dr. Phillips smiled again and in Renee's present state of agitation it was like gasoline on a fire. "Please stop smiling at me like that. Like you know something I don't. Don't you understand? I'm bad news. And John doesn't need or want the kind of complications I bring to the table. I'm talking major baggage. The kind you should have to declare before you board the relationship airplane."

"And you think he doesn't realize this?"

"Of course he doesn't," Renee snapped. "If he did he'd run far and fast."

"And he's not."

"No." Was that her voice that sounded just a bit mournful? Renee bit her lip to fight the inexplicable tears that filled her eyes. "No, he's not."

"Maybe he sees something in you that he likes and

that makes him willing to shoulder your 'baggage' as you call it."

Renee snorted. "Like what? A recovering alcoholic with a loser ex-husband who could show up at any moment, and three little girls, one of whom can't seem to stand me, and barely tolerates anyone else. Oh, yes. I'm a prime package. Who wouldn't want to take me on?"

"Renee," Dr. Phillips leaned forward. "Anyone can change the course of their life. Just as you did when you chose sobriety. When you chose to find your girls no matter what. When you chose to stick it through even though Alexis is not making it easy. You don't give yourself enough credit. John is an adult. He doesn't need you to protect him from whatever he might choose to take on."

Renee hated the logic of that statement. It stripped away her carefully constructed excuses as if they were made from thin strips of gauze and Renee was left with nothing but the ruin of it in her hands. Silence filled the room.

"It was more than sex," Renee admitted quietly. "I'm pretty sure I fell in love with him." Even before the sex happened. Possibly the moment she realized he'd protect her girls from everyone…including herself.

"You aren't sure?"

Renee twisted the strap on her purse and refused to meet the doctor's gaze. The inquiry in her voice was enough to make her cheeks burn. Of course she knew.

It was just so mortifying to admit. Who falls in love within such a short time under these kinds of conditions? It practically screamed *dysfunction* and Renee was doing her best to avoid that kind of—

"Has he fallen in love with you?" The doctor broke into Renee's thoughts.

She swallowed. "I don't know."

"And if he has?"

Her heart stuttered painfully and while the possibility filled her soul with ridiculous misplaced hope that a future with John might be in her grasp, the cold hand of reality slapped her hard and fast and she forced the next words out of her mouth.

"Then he's not as smart as I gave him credit for. There's absolutely no future between John and me. I hate it here and I'm leaving as soon as I get the green light. How's that for the possibility of happily ever after?"

"Renee—"

Tears blinded her and she ran out of the office before Dr. Phillips could call her bluff and see the very thing Renee wanted to hide from everyone—including herself—and that was the fact that she'd fallen hard for the very man that she should've kept her distance from.

RENEE WASN'T THINKING CLEARLY. She drove like a madwoman to the house, one thing on her mind. Get out. Leave. Run.

Bursting into the house, she started calling for the girls, startling Gladys in the process.

"Goodness gracious, what's all the fuss for?" Gladys asked, trailing Renee with a worried frown. "You look like you've seen a ghost or something. Therapy not go well today?"

Renee ignored Gladys's question, intent on finding her girls. She found them in their bedroom with Alexis at the small desk doing homework and Taylor looking at a horse picture book with Chloe.

Wiping at the tears flowing down her cheeks, Renee went to the closet and started pulling clothes from the racks.

Gladys, hands on her hips, exclaimed, "Child, have you done lost your mind? What are you doing?"

"Leaving."

Alexis jumped up from her chair and fairly screeched at the top of her lungs, "No, we're not! And you can't make us! The court says—"

"I'm your mother! And I say we're leaving!"

Gladys paled and disappeared. Renee knew where she was going and panic fueled her thoughts. Kneeling before Alexis, she implored her oldest child. "Please, sweetheart. This isn't the place for us. This isn't real! The longer we stay the harder it will be to leave. Don't you realize that? We don't belong here. It's not our house. Not our family. We're all we have and we have to stick together. Please…please…" Her plea ended in a pained whisper and Chloe began to wail.

"Don't wanna go," she sniffed as Taylor hugged her close with wide, fearful eyes. "Don't wanna g-go."

Renee felt her heart crack as she looked at her

children, their frightened faces searing into her brain, just as John skidded around the corner with Gladys on his tail. Brokenhearted and defeated, Renee dropped her face into her hands and started to sob.

The next thing Renee knew, she was in John's arms.

JOHN HELD RENEE AS SHE CRIED what seemed like an endless stream of tears. When Gladys had come running to him in a panic, he'd simply reacted. But then as Renee had folded in on herself, he couldn't stop himself from going to her.

Leaving Gladys to calm the girls, he took Renee to the bedroom and closed the door for privacy.

After a long while, her sobs turned to watery hiccups and John felt her take a deep, shuddering breath.

"You probably think I'm insane," she said against his chest.

"The thought did occur to me," he said mildly.

"You wouldn't be far off," she said, pulling away and wiping at her face with the flat of her palm. "I feel like I'm being torn in two."

"How so?"

She sighed. "Because."

"Because why?"

She looked him square in the eye. "What's going on between us?"

The tender and protective feelings he'd felt moments earlier faded to wariness. "You said it yourself. Release."

She swallowed. "What if I was wrong?" She whispered the words as if afraid of saying them aloud.

It's the same damn question he'd been asking himself since that night. He'd always considered himself a simple man but since meeting Renee, his life had been turned upside down and everything he'd thought was black and white were really shades of gray. He shared the same insecurities as she did, it's just that he didn't wear his feelings on his sleeve for everyone to see.

"Do you…have feelings for me?" she asked.

The simple answer? Yes. But it wasn't as simple as that and he wasn't fool enough to believe that. Instead of answering, he pointed out, "You hate it here. So what difference does it make if I do have feelings for you? My life is here. I'm not going anywhere."

"I know."

"So…"

She hung her head, the corners of her mouth pulling down. "So, the very thing that I didn't want to happen, has happened and I don't know what to do about it."

John thought about what she was implying but he didn't have the courage to ask her to clarify. Did he want to know? He sensed she was talking about more than the physical act they shared. She wasn't the only one dealing with a barrage of inappropriate feelings. She was the last person he wanted to have feelings for. Renee was like a stick of dynamite, dangerous and ready to explode at any minute. John liked routine whereas Renee seemed to balk at anything smacking of customary. He'd been a bachelor for so long…he just didn't know if he was capable of becoming a husband and a father in one fell swoop, but the thought of watching the girls and Renee walk away and never come back took a chunk out of his heart.

"Wow. This sucks," Renee said wryly, her voice nasal from the crying jag. He chuckled but it sounded as hollow as he felt. She drew a deep breath and apologized for her earlier behavior. "I don't know what came over me. Tough day at therapy I guess."

He nodded but felt it safer to remain silent. There was too much going on in his head to trust what might come out of his mouth. He couldn't help but wonder what chink in Renee's armor had allowed such a breakdown. Something had obviously hit a nerve. A part of him needed to know. The other part shied away from the knowledge. She stood and he didn't try to stop her.

"I'd like to say that I'm never this irrational but the truth of the matter is…I have days where I don't do anything that makes sense. That's what scares me. I'm trying to change that part of myself and you seem to bring out that particular trait in me. I have to steer clear of any self-destructive patterns. Not just for my girls…but for myself. You understand, right?"

He did. Everything she said made perfect sense and he should've just nodded and agreed because essentially they were on the same page, but his heart was singing a different tune and the sound of it was drowning out the melody of reason.

IT'D BEEN SEVERAL DAYS since The Day Renee Lost Her Mind as Alexis liked to call it, and although Renee wished she wouldn't say that, she had to admire her daughter's wry sense of humor about the whole humiliating episode.

Renee was sitting outside on the porch swing watching John in the arena as he worked with Vixen when Gladys came out to join her with a hot mug of cider.

"He's something else with that horse," Gladys remarked mildly and Renee agreed, somewhat in awe of John in his environment. Something akin to wonder and pride swelled her heart even though she shouldn't indulge in such fanciful emotions. Gladys shook her head. "But then he's always been something of a miracle worker when it comes to animals. When he was a boy he used to give his mama fits for all the critters he'd bring home and stash in his room. Lizards, birds, squirrels…anything that needed his help. It was just his way."

The older woman handed Renee the mug and sat in the old wicker chair and sipped her hot drink in silence. Renee felt terrible for scaring Gladys that day. In the short time she'd gotten to know Gladys, she felt closer to the older woman than she had to her own mother.

"I'm sorry."

"I know you are."

Renee smiled above her mug. "Were you always this wise or did it come with age?"

"I've always been smarter than the average bear,"

Gladys answered cheekily, eliciting a chuckle from Renee. They settled into a companionable silence until Gladys brought up the one subject Renee wanted to stay away from. "I know you're in love with John." Renee started to protest but Gladys motioned for her to be quiet and listen. "John is a good man. Better than most I'd say. You're never going to find a man as solid and dependable and loving than that man right there. What more are you looking for, child?"

"What makes you think I'm looking at all?"

"It's in your eyes. You yearn for happiness and sta-bility and that's not a bad thing. Why else would you have stayed with that good-for-nothing nephew of mine? You were trying to make a go of it even when you knew it was falling apart at the seams. A woman doesn't do that when she's hoping and wishing to be footloose and fancy-free."

"Gladys, I wish I could say that was the case but it wasn't. I stayed because I was a drunk and a failure. Where else was I supposed to go?"

"Stop that." Gladys's normal tone sharpened with her annoyance. "Everyone makes mistakes. It's how you deal with those mistakes that make up the strength of your backbone. You didn't run away from your girls. You went to get help for yourself first so you could take care of them properly. You couldn't have known that Jason was going to fly the coop or do something to Chloe. If you had, I know you wouldn't have left them behind. Stop beating yourself up, child."

If only it were that simple. "Alexis…she's never going to forgive me."

"She will. But it'll take time. She loves you something fierce. Trust me in this if nothing else."

Tears stung Renee's eyes. "I miss her." *Desperately.* Renee hadn't realized how much she depended on her oldest daughter until she fell into the void left by her absence. It also made her realize that she'd put entirely too much pressure on the child and somewhere along the way Alexis had lost her childhood. How could Renee give it back to her?

"And she misses you. Don't give up. She'll come around when she senses she can trust you. But you know, the problem isn't with Alexis or John."

"Oh?" Renee wiped at her eyes. "What is the problem then?"

Gladys pointed and tapped Renee gently in the chest where her heart beat painfully. "It's here."

"What do you mean?" Renee asked, though to be truthful she was afraid of what Gladys was going to say. Part of her already knew.

"Honey, you're afraid of opening up and letting go of that part of yourself that keeps you believing that you're not worthy of a good life."

"Why wouldn't I want to let go of that?" Renee asked, half joking, despite the look in Gladys's eyes that was anything but full of laughter.

"That's something you have to ask yourself, child. When you find that answer, everything else will fall into place."

CHAPTER SEVENTEEN

JOHN WAS ON A SHORT FUSE the day Cutter Buford returned to collect his horse and Cutter's attitude didn't improve matters.

It had taken weeks to get Vixen to the point where she would tolerate John—and no one else—but Cutter wasn't pleased that his expensive horseflesh clearly seemed to hate him. Her nostrils flared and she neighed sharply as she punched the ground with her front hooves.

"What's this shit?" Cutter yelled, jumping away from Vixen and out of the arena as John followed. "I paid you good money to tame this horse! She doesn't look any different than when I brought her to you."

"She doesn't like you," John said, unwilling to sugarcoat anything for this dumb-ass abusive man. "I can't change that. For what it's worth, she doesn't act up around me."

"Well that doesn't do me any good, now does it?" he sneered, sucking back a wad of spit before letting it fly at John's feet. "I paid you good money and all I get for it is 'she don't like you'? I want my money and my horse back you son of a bitch. Now."

John wasn't impressed or intimidated by Cutter's bluster but he was interested in one thing. "Let me buy her off you," he suggested.

"Excuse me?"

"You said it yourself, she's no good to you if you can't ride her. She's not likely to ever take a shine to you seeing as you abused her." Cutter's face turned florid at the accusation but John wasn't finished. "That's right. Abused. You're out of your mind if you think I can't recognize the signs."

"Watch what you're saying," Cutter warned. "I don't take kindly to being accused of beating my horses."

"And I don't take kindly to someone bringing me a horse they've mistreated and then threatening to put me out of business because I couldn't fix what you broke."

Cutter's jaw clenched and then ordered his horse loaded.

"What are you going to do with her?" John asked.

Cutter threw a dark look his way. "I'd say that's none of your business."

"Perhaps. But let me tell you one more thing. I filed a report with the Sheriff's Department about my suspicions and took pictures of the odd wounds that were on her flank when she arrived. Don't be surprised if you get a call. Who knows, they might find cause to poke around your stables and make sure the rest of your horses aren't suffering from the same type of *treatment*."

John was mildly concerned that Cutter was going to drop dead from a heart attack as the man's face went three different shades of red during the course of their short conversation but the truth was, John knew if he didn't persuade Cutter to cut Vixen loose, Cutter was going to more than likely put a bullet between her eyes. He was a cruel son of a bitch and John had grown fond of the cantankerous horse.

"Sell her to me and we'll conclude our business together," John said, a thread of steel in his tone.

Cutter paused, clearly torn between wanting to storm out of there in a cloud of dust and taking the money for a horse he would never be able to ride. In the end, greed won out and for that John was grateful for the man's baser instincts.

Biting out an exorbitant sum, John countered with a more acceptable one and Cutter, knowing he was still coming out on the plus side, accepted.

Cutter sent one last ugly look at Vixen and said, "You two deserve each other. I hope she breaks your neck."

John laughed at that and flipped Cutter off as he drove away. As Gladys would say, "Good riddance to bad rubbish." And damn if that wasn't the truth.

Out of nowhere, Taylor jumped into his arms like a monkey and rained kisses on his wind-chapped cheeks. "I knew you wouldn't let Vixen go to that bad man! I just knew it!"

His heart warmed at Taylor's unabashed adoration and he hugged her tight. He turned to walk to the house and caught Renee watching him and Taylor with a soft look in her eyes. If Taylor's belief in him warmed him, Renee's look started a fire deep inside. A man could spend a lifetime basking in the heat of that stare, he realized.

Shaken, he offered a lopsided smile as he approached.

"Renee, Mr. John bought Vixen so she never has to leave the ranch." She cocked her head. "Do you think Mr. John could buy us so we could stay, too?"

Renee laughed and the sound was something he wished he could bottle up and savor. He was losing his damn mind over a woman, but the funny thing?—he didn't care as much as he thought he would.

"I'M THINKING OF INVITING my brother and his family over for dinner. How do you feel about that?" John asked casually the following evening. Renee looked up from her crossword with a startled expression.

"Oh, sure. Do you want me and the girls to cut out for the evening? We could go for pizza or something I guess."

"No." He shook his head. "I'd like you and the girls to stay."

She looked uncertain and he knew how she felt. He felt the same but he wanted Evan to meet her. His younger brother was the only person's opinion he trusted more than Gladys's, and right now he could use all the help he could get in sorting out the mess that was going on in his head.

RENEE WAS A NERVOUS WRECK. Why did she agree to this? She should've flat out refused. She had no business meeting his family. That just tangled an already confusing situation. But she'd be a liar if she wasn't touched by his desire to open up to her like that. From what she'd learned of John he was an intensely private person and he rarely invited any woman into the inner sanctum of his life. So what did it mean that he was inviting her and the girls? Well, it wasn't so much about the girls. She already knew he'd fallen in love with them. Not that that was hard. Her daughters were pretty awesome but what did that say about her? Was he falling for her? He'd never actually said the words to her and she wasn't about to put money on a feeling or a hunch.

Voices carried from the living room and Renee knew she couldn't hide in the bathroom forever. Smoothing her western-style skirt she'd purchased in town, she gave one final look at her hair in the mirror and noted in despair that it was springing free from the fashion clip she'd tried to use, and with an exasperated sigh she pulled it free. Ruffing her hair for some lift, she just hoped for the best and left the bathroom.

She rounded the corner from the hallway to see a very blond family getting out of their overcoats. Evan and his wife shared nearly the same shade of blond as one another and there were two young boys with only slightly different shades of blond bounding around the room. Taylor was squealing with delight at their antics.

"You must be Renee." The blond woman came

toward Renee with a warm, inviting smile that immediately put Renee at ease as she accepted a handshake
in welcome. "I'm Natalie. That man over there is my
husband, Evan, and those little monsters tearing up the
living room are our sons, Colton and Justin. Your girls
are beautiful. But it's no wonder, just look at their
mother."

Renee blushed but loved the compliment for her
daughters' sake. She took pride in her daughters and
knew they were all quite pretty. "Thank you. Your sons
aren't hard on the eyes, either," Renee said in return.

Natalie smiled and then the boys, who looked
roughly two years apart, with the younger looking to
be close to the same age as Chloe, took off for the rec
room. Moments later the sounds of cue balls smacking
into one another were heard followed by laughter.

"Seems they've hit it off," Natalie observed, then
gestured toward the kitchen. "Let's go see if Gladys
needs any help. Did she ever tell you she's the reason
I met Evan in the first place?"

"Um, no, I don't think so." Renee followed, intrigued
by this personal history. "But I'd love to hear that story."

"Well, I got duped into going white-water rafting
and Gladys was the first person I met on the trip, aside
from Evan, who was the river guide. Long story short,
we met and now that I look back, I realize it was love
at first sight. Oh, and then I got pregnant."

That shocked a laugh out of Renee. "Love at first
sight, huh? You sure it wasn't just baby hormones?"

"Oh, I tried to tell myself that at first because I

wasn't planning to be a mom or a wife at the time but things happened as they should have and I'm so glad."

They reached the kitchen and after a lot of exclaiming and hugging between the two women, Gladys enlisted the help of both Renee and Natalie to put the finishing touches on dinner.

Renee silently marveled at the easy camaraderie between the two women as well as the obvious love and she couldn't help but compare the relationships she'd had in her life even though it was like comparing apples to oranges. She'd never known female companionship such as this. Not with friends, certainly not with her mother. The closest she'd ever come to something like this was the brief relationship she'd shared with her elderly aunt Katherine. Aunt Kat, as she'd liked to be called. Melancholy followed the precious few memories she had of Aunt Kat, which was why Renee rarely called them up.

Then her thoughts wandered to her girls and what kind of relationships they've had in their lives. Alexis had been right when she'd said they'd moved around a lot. Sustaining ties wasn't something the Dolling family had excelled at. Jason had a tendency to get itchy like a caged animal if they stayed in one place for too long. Plus, it was true, just about the time Jason was ready to get out of Dodge, was about the same time their luck had run out with local creditors. Renee came out of the morass of her own thoughts when she realized Natalie was asking her a question.

"I'm sorry…what did you say?" Renee asked, embarrassed to be caught in her own head like that. "I didn't catch what you said."

"Oh, it was nothing. Gladys and I got to talking about my sisters and what they've been up to and I asked if you had any sisters or brothers."

"No. Single child. I wish I'd had siblings, though," Renee said, which was true. She'd always hoped for a sibling, if only to take the pressure from herself. Bearing the weight of her parents' hopes and dreams all by herself had been a little daunting. "But it was just me."

"I can vouch for having sisters. I'd be lost without them," Natalie said and Gladys chuckled knowingly. "Oh, don't get me wrong. They drive me crazy but it's nice to always have someone in your corner."

"I bet," Renee murmured, thinking of her daughters and how close they were. She smiled in spite of the lingering pain that ghosted her heart when she thought of her girls and what they'd been through. "I'm glad my girls have each other."

Natalie nodded, then as she brought the salad bowl to the table, her eyes took on an interested sparkle as she asked the one thing Renee didn't know how to answer without ruining the whole evening. "So, I'm a little unclear…how did you and John meet?"

Renee thought hard on how to answer. She didn't want to destroy the nice impression Natalie had of her but then again, she didn't want to lie, either. She glanced at Gladys as if looking for guidance and she received an encouraging smile. Taking a deep breath, Renee said, "I lost custody of my girls, and Gladys and John are taking care of them for me until I can get them back. That's all."

"Oh." Natalie looked nonplussed. "But I thought you and John were…dating."

"No. He's just being a good Samaritan."

"Well, he's definitely good at that. Hmm, well, it's nice to meet you just the same. I'd hoped for something a little more, to be truthful. From what I know of John, he's never let a stranger move into his space without a good reason and the only reason I could imagine was that he'd finally fallen in love." Natalie huffed a disappointed sigh. "Well, I guess it's true. I'm such a hopeless romantic."

Renee smiled and secretly wished Natalie had been right. She wanted John to want her—not just the girls—in his life. And the knowledge that she still yearned for something so foreign and quite possibly out of reach was disturbing.

JOHN TOOK EVAN OUT TO THE BARN to see his newly acquired horse after sharing the circumstances as to how the mare came into his possession. Then the brothers chitchatted about nothing for a while until John got around to broaching the subject he needed his brother's opinion on.

"She seems like a passionate woman," Evan remarked to John's surprise.

"What makes you say that?"

"I can see it in her eyes. She was holding back at dinner. Am I wrong?"

John thought of Renee throughout dinner and how reserved she seemed and he had to agree. "No. You're right. Something was weighing on her mind tonight. No doubt she was nervous about meeting you and Natalie. She's been judged pretty harshly by people recently. I think maybe she was afraid you guys might judge her, too."

"I hope she knows after tonight that we're not like that," Evan said seriously.

"I think she does."

"Good. I like her," Evan announced.

John looked at his brother. "You do? No reservation? Even after what I told you? With the kids and the ex and all that?"

"People make mistakes. She seems to be a good person. You could do a lot worse."

"What makes you think I'm interested in her in that way?" John bluffed, silently chafing that Evan could read him so easily. He was the older brother, for crying out loud, yet Evan seemed the wiser at the moment. Had to be Natalie's influence, thought John peevishly, but then in all fairness to Evan he had to admit that fatherhood had treated Evan well, rounding out the rough edges until he was a man to be proud of. "She's a handful," John admitted.

"The best ones usually are."

"What if I'm not ready to be a father and a husband?"

Evan chuckled. "Seems to me like you're already playing the part, minus a few details here and there."

"I've been a bachelor for a long time," he reminded Evan. "I might not be able to change to accommodate an instant family."

At that Evan laughed aloud. "Brother, you're kidding yourself. You've already changed. Those girls have you wrapped around their finger. Face it…you're in love."

John grunted. There was no sense in denying it. He did love those girls. But what about Renee? He knew the answer to that, too, but couldn't seem to admit it just yet.

"She's leaving as soon as the court awards custody," he said, his heart contracting at the very thought. "She's pretty vocal about that. Can't stand living in the country. She's going to go back to where it doesn't snow and it's one hundred degrees in the shade."

"How much more time before the court awards custody?"

John's mouth pulled at the corners. "Not long. Two weeks, I suppose. We have another court hearing coming up."

Evan surprised him with a hearty thump on the back. "Then I suggest if you don't want to lose all of them you better get to work finding a way to make this place somewhere Renee would happily call home."

"And how do you suppose I do that?" John asked dourly. "Offer to paint? New wallpaper?"

Evan laughed. "That would be your problem. I can't do everything for you. Isn't that what you used to tell me when I'd get myself into a scrap? Damn, it feels good to finally be able to say that to you."

He gave John a wide grin and John couldn't help but return it before muttering, "If that's the extent of your wisdom let's get back to the house before we freeze our asses off."

CHAPTER EIGHTEEN

ALEXIS SAT AS FAR AWAY from Renee as she could, on the farthest edge of the sofa, but at least she wasn't glaring at her, thought Renee, trying to cling to any semblance of progress with her daughter.

It was the second integration therapy between her and Alexis and the first one had been a disaster, not that Renee had expected much else. But Renee was willing to do anything to bridge the gap between them, even if that meant more sessions with Dr. Phillips, which frankly set her teeth on edge.

"Alexis…did you bring your letter?" Dr. Phillips inquired gently. Alexis gave a faint nod. Renee nearly let out a whoosh of breath she'd been holding. Dr. Phillips looked to Renee. "Renee…did you bring yours?"

Renee nodded and pulled a folded up piece of paper from her purse.

"Excellent. Now this is how it will work. Last week I gave you both an assignment. You were to write a letter to the person you are most hurt by and tell them all the things you are sorry for and all the things that you feel the other person should apologize for." She held up a finger to silence Alexis before she could interject something caustic and continued in her soft voice. "This is a safe place. When you are reading your letter there will be no interruptions from the other party. This is about healing and listening."

Renee's palms felt sweaty but she waited for Dr. Phillips.

Alexis shot Renee an uncertain look before turning to Dr. Phillips. "Do I have to go first?" she asked in a small, hard voice.

"Only if you want to."

"I don't."

Dr. Phillips nodded and turned to Renee. "Then Renee shall go first. You don't mind, do you?"

Renee shook her head and lifted her letter so she could read it, although tears were already clogging her throat as she cleared it. She started, only to stop and have to start again before she could get her mouth to cooperate.

"My darling, sweet Alexis. I am deeply sorry that I put you in a position where you had to be the parent because I couldn't be. Your father and I took your childhood away from you with our selfish behavior and I can't change the past but I can give you a better future if you'll let me. I am so sorry for the missed birthday parties, the constant moving around and the burden we placed on you at such a young age. Even though

I thought I was doing the right thing, I never should've left you and the babies behind with your father. I should've realized he was unstable. His drug use had gotten out of control but I was panicked. I couldn't stay there a minute longer without doing something crazy and in a moment of pure desperation I put myself before my children. I'll spend the rest of my life regretting that choice. Every night Chloe screams in her sleep it rips my heart out. Every time I see that frightened look in Taylor's eyes I want to cry but worse…every time I see that cold, hateful expression in your eyes when you look at me, I cringe because I know I deserve it."

Renee paused a minute to gauge Alexis's reaction and was bolstered by the silent yet wide-eyed look as her oldest daughter listened. She continued.

"Alexis…my golden girl. My soldier. Child of my heart. I can never explain the depth of my love for you. It's bottomless. I can only hope that someday when you're holding your own child in your arms you'll understand the depth of what I feel for you. Until then, I just want the privilege of being your mother. If you'll just let me in, I promise I'll never let you down again."

Renee wiped her eyes and slowly folded her letter. Dr. Phillips gestured to Alexis, encouraging her gently. "It's your turn, sweetheart. Say what you need to say to your mom."

Alexis turned her blue eyes to Dr. Phillips as if pleading with her but when the doctor simply offered a smile of encouragement, Alexis pulled a crumpled piece of paper from her pocket and smoothed it out so she could read it. Swallowing hard, she began in a small voice.

"I'm mad at you for running away and not taking us with you and leaving us with Daddy. I'm mad because I tried to be the best daughter but you left anyway. You left us all behind and then you didn't find us in time before Daddy hurt Chloe. I'm mad because I couldn't stop him from putting her outside in the rain. I'm mad because you didn't love us more than you loved your drinks. I'm mad because—"

Alexis stopped long enough to suck back a watery hiccup,

"—you said you'd never leave us and you did. You left us behind. Why?"

That last part came out a pained whisper and Renee felt her heart splinter in a million pieces.

"I do love you," she whispered back. "I do. So much."

Alexis wiped a sleeve across her running nose and her eyes were red-rimmed and glassy. "I don't believe you."

"I know. But I will gladly spend the rest of my life showing you how much I've changed if you'd just let me try."

"What if you leave again?"

"I won't." Renee made that a solemn promise.

"What if you start drinking again?"

Renee took a deep breath. She wouldn't lie to her daughter. "Every day is a struggle not to drink but I am committed to sobriety. I haven't slipped yet and every day that I don't drink is a victory that I celebrate. It's one day at a time, sweetheart. That's the only promise I can make."

"Alexis…do you miss your mom?"

Her small bottom lip quivered, giving away the answer even though Alexis remained silent. Then, Alexis looked to Dr. Phillips and nodded.

"Then tell her."

Alexis slowly met Renee's gaze and time seemed to stop for Renee as her daughter struggled to get out the words that seemed trapped in her small chest. But finally Renee heard the words that she so longed to hear and nearly collapsed from the weight of it.

"I miss you…Mom."

Renee didn't wait and scooped her daughter into her arms, clutching her young body to her own as if it were a lifeline to heaven and her own sobs mingled with Alexis's. She whispered into her hair, inhaling deep the sweet scent of her child as she clung to her, "I will never let you down again. Ever."

And that was a promise she'd never break.

JOHN NOTICED THE DIFFERENCE in Alexis the moment she and Renee returned from their therapy session. There was a tentative peacefulness that hadn't been there previously. A weight fell from his shoulders as he realized they must've turned a corner together. He was glad. It hurt him to see Alexis so twisted up inside over this thing with her mother.

But even as he was happy for Renee, his mind was turning in circles over what was soon to come. Their court date was fast approaching, which meant it was likely the judge was going to rule in Renee's favor. And he should. She was a good mother and she deserved her children back. If only it didn't hurt like hell to think of how empty his house and his life would be with their absence.

He was accustomed to his little shadow out in the barn as Taylor never missed a morning to get up and help him before she went off to school, no matter how early or cold. She was an endless source of entertainment with her playful antics and unique slant on things. She was more like him than he would've ever deemed possible even though they shared no blood. Alexis was a beauty he knew would need someone to watch out for her when the boys started to realize just how pretty she was. He wanted to be around to make sure that she was treated right by any boy who happened to catch her eye and heaven help any kid who made her cry. And Chloe…a perpetually soft spot was held for that sunny kid. The other day she'd called him Daddy. He'd kept it to himself but it had affected him in a powerful way. He didn't correct her though he knew he should've.

Of course, it all came down to Renee, though. She dominated his thoughts morning and night. His hungry gaze sought her out and feasted whenever he found her. Her fair beauty, wonderful curves and hearty laughter made him grin like a silly boy.

For the first time in his life, he knew what it was like to pine for someone who was out of his reach. Before he realized it, he'd left the arena and had wandered to Renee's cottage. He meant to stop and turn around once he realized where he was headed but his feet weren't listening any more than his heart was and soon he was knocking on her door.

She opened it and offered him an unsure smile. "The girls okay?"

"They're fine. Doing homework and eating cookies. Can I come in for a minute?"

"Sure." She held the door open wider and he moved past her, their bodies touching briefly and electrifying the space between them.

"Things go well at therapy?"

She smiled. "Actually, I can't believe I'm going to say this but yes, it did go well. I think Alexis and I are going to be okay."

"I'm glad."

"Any problems with that Cutter guy since buying Vixen?" she asked.

He shook his head. "He's a puss. Sheriff Casey paid him a visit a few days ago and a little bird told me that he might be leaving town. Just doesn't fit in, I guess."

"It's hard to fit in with a small town," Renee murmured. "Outsiders…they aren't exactly welcomed with open arms around here."

"For people like Cutter Buford, you're right. But if you're talking about yourself, you're wrong. This town would embrace you if you let them."

She looked at him and he read a wealth of insecurity there. Finally, she shook her head sadly. "I'm not small-town girl material. Even if I wish I were."

That last part came out a soft whisper that twisted his heart in wicked knots.

"You could be," he said.

"What would I do here? I can't continue to be your housekeeper. What would happen to me and my girls when you meet someone you want to settle down with? I'm tired of having a throwaway future."

He wanted to tell her that he'd found the person he wanted to settle down with but his damn mouth wouldn't cooperate. She was set on leaving. Who was he to try and convince her otherwise? Seemed an exercise doomed to fail in his book. He gave a curt nod as if he understood and perhaps even agreed when in fact he was just afraid of being rejected. He really didn't have all that much practice with putting his heart on the line. He didn't know what to say or do to make it right for the both of them.

Instead he changed subjects. "Are you nervous about court?" he asked.

She risked a small smile but it looked ragged on the edges as she admitted, "Yes. Very."

"Don't be," he assured her roughly. "You've done all the right things. You deserve to get your girls back."

Her eyes warmed with gratitude and it nearly knocked him over. She grasped his hand tightly. "Thank you. For everything you've done for my girls...and for me. I can never repay you."

He wanted to shuck off her gratitude knowing that he selfishly wanted to do anything to hold on to them, but he merely accepted her thanks with another short nod before grasping the door handle to leave.

"John..."

He turned. "Yeah?"

Her eyes shone with a soft light that he'd happily go blind from and it seemed she yearned for him to say something to fill the space between them, but the odd ache in his chest was making it difficult to think clearly. Crossing to him, she wrapped her arms around him and he automatically reciprocated, sheltering her within his arms as her lips found his in a tender, soul-searing kiss that rocked him to his toes.

He gripped her tightly, afraid to let go, afraid to continue. Slanting his mouth greedily over hers, he was tempted to devour her for the need fueling his blood. He'd never get enough. In a million years he'd never have his fill of this woman. Her body molded to his in perfect symmetry like two pieces of a puzzle locking together and he wondered how he'd ever thought he'd been in love before this moment. He knew this was love because he'd watch her walk away if he knew that would make her happy.

Pulling away slowly, he memorized the features of her face. Then with a final crack of his heart, he made his voice take on a light tone as if what had just happened between them hadn't just laid bare every emotion he was capable of feeling, and he said, "A simple thank you would've been fine."

Her expression dimmed and she looked at him with open hurt for his flippant comment. "Why do you have to do that?"

He sighed and tugged at his baseball cap. "Renee… we always knew this day would come. I've never been one for long goodbyes and obviously I'm no good at this stuff."

"You don't have to make it worse," she said coldly.

"You're right. I'm sorry."

That seemed to mollify her slightly and she nodded. Without much else to say that wouldn't inadvertently make things worse between them, John let himself out.

TOMORROW WAS HER COURT DATE and she was all packed and ready to go. She knew there was a slim possibility that the judge might not rule in her favor but she'd been in contact with her social worker and since Alexis's turn-around in therapy, she had reason to hope for a good resolution. By tomorrow, she and her girls could leave this place behind and everything it entailed.

So why did her heart feel like lead in her chest? Sinking her head into her hands as she plopped down on the edge of the bed, she exhaled loudly and wanted to groan.

She just needed space to think. Once she and the girls were settled somewhere else without John around to cloud their judgment things would clear up. She avoided thinking about how upset the girls would be when she told them they were leaving. Alexis knew the court date was coming yet she had remained silent, knowing as well that the little girls wouldn't understand why they couldn't stay. Renee wasn't sure if Alexis understood, either, but she was placing her trust in Renee to do what was right for them.

That was it, though. Right now, Renee didn't know what was right. If she listened to her traitorous heart the right thing was to stay here with John and build a life in the sticks even though that went against every thing she thought she wanted. If she listened to her head and consequently her pride, the right thing was to get in the car and drive far, far away and try to blot out the memory of ever being here. The girls would adapt and everything would be fine.

Easier said than done. Her heart already wailed at the thought of walking out that door and never coming back. She'd miss John in a way that was palpable.

How'd that happen? Sneaky man with his handsome face and rough disposition, she groused. Slapping the bedspread and causing dust motes to float lazily into the stream of sunlight coming through the window, she was nowhere closer to finding the truth of her feelings than she was when she started asking questions.

Here's what it came down to: Did she love John Murphy? The kind of love that was gritty and messy and strong and wonderful? Or was this a fleeting infatuation that would eventually weaken under the strain of everyday living?

She thought of John with her girls and her heart filled with love for his willing sacrifice. She thought of John with Gladys and his deep feelings for an older woman who wasn't his blood and respect blossomed. And lastly, she thought of John the night they made love and she had her answer.

So why did that make her want to cry?

CHAPTER NINETEEN

THE DAY OF COURT BROKE with bright rays of yellow sunshine and birds chirping as if it weren't the worst day of John's life.

Showering quickly, he told himself it was better to get this over with than drag it out. He knew Renee hadn't told the girls that today was the day they might leave and he knew why she was reluctant. The news wasn't likely to go over very well. He didn't begrudge her wanting to put off that moment for as long as she could. Besides, there was always a slim chance the judge might want a little more time to decide. The flicker of hope he felt at that possibility filled him with guilt. It was plain selfish to think that way and he was instantly ashamed for even considering it. Renee deserved her children and he wouldn't say or do a thing to keep them from her.

She'd come a long way from the woman he'd first seen that cold winter day. He didn't even recognize her as the same person. There was no way he could've seen the true woman hiding behind that angry facade that first day. He wondered how things might've been different if he had…shaking off the useless direction of his thoughts he trained his focus on his breakfast, not trusting his own mouth to remain buttoned without something to keep it busy.

In spite of the sunny day the morning was promising to turn into, the house had a pall over it that only the adults seemed to notice. The girls got ready for school just as they always did. Chloe sat at the breakfast table eating her cereal while Gladys and Renee made lunches for the two older girls.

"Bye, Mom!" Alexis and Taylor said in unison as they grabbed their lunch sacks and ran for the door as the sound of the school bus rumbled down the road. It was all so damn normal and appealing that John had to blink back an odd moisture in his eyes.

"What time is court?" Gladys asked once the older girls were gone and Chloe had scampered off to watch her favorite early morning cartoons.

"Eight-thirty," Renee answered, shooting a vulnerable look John's way.

"Then you'd better get going, I suppose," Gladys said, her voice tinged with sadness. She hugged Renee tightly and offered good luck. To John she said, "You driving?"

He looked at Renee and she shrugged. "Sure," he answered, though his chest felt tight.

They drove in silence until John couldn't take it any longer. Desperation had started to set in and all he could think of was that he was about to lose the people in his life that had come to mean the most.

"Renee—"

Suddenly Renee twisted to stare out the window to the vehicle that had just barreled past them and she cut him off with a shriek. "Oh my God! That was Jason!"

Everything else forgotten, he looked at Renee sharply. "Are you sure?"

"I'm positive. He's headed for Gladys's house and Gladys mentioned that she and Chloe were going to go and water her plants this morning. Turn around, turn around!"

Wrenching the wheel, John chewed up the gravel on the shoulder and punched the gas to head back where they'd came.

"Why is he coming back? What does he want?" she asked, clearly talking to herself. The panic in her voice mirroring the growing rage that was building inside him if that man so much as touched a hair on Chloe's head. "Thank God the older girls are at school," she said to John and he agreed. The less they witnessed the better off they'd be. John had a feeling things were about to get ugly. She turned to him, clutching at his shirtsleeve with wide, frightened eyes. "What if he tries to take Chloe to get back at me or he forces Gladys to tell him where his girls go to school? Oh, God…why is he doing this? Why couldn't he just stay gone!"

"There's a restraining order filed against him, barring him from contact with the girls or coming onto the ranch and there's a warrant out for his arrest. He's not going anywhere."

"Pieces of paper aren't going to stop Jason if he wants to take them," Renee said. "He's never had any respect for the law, he's not about to start now."

"We'll see about that." Flipping open his cell phone, he dialed Sheriff Casey's cell phone. "John here. That SOB is back and he's headed for Gladys's place. Send a deputy if you want things handled your way. We were on our way to court when we passed him on the highway. He's driving a beat-up silver Nissan with Arizona plates."

"Jason is unstable," Renee told John in a thready voice tinged with true fear. "He was always a bit of a wild card…it's part of what attracted me the most," she added in a shameful whisper. He couldn't help but wonder if that sort of thing was still what turned her clock but his question must've planted itself in his expression because she shook her head decisively. "Not now. Back when I was a stupid, rebellious kid. I've had enough of that kind of excitement. But right now…I want to plant my fist in Jason's face."

"You and me both," John muttered darkly. God help the man if they got there before the deputies. The way John figured it, he and good ol' Jason had a few things to settle.

"He might take Chloe for leverage," Renee said suddenly, the furrow in her brow deepening with pain. "He's used the kids against me before. He'd do it again. Oh, God, John, please don't let him hurt my baby again."

"He won't touch her." That was a promise.

GLADYS WAS IN THE PROCESS of watering her spider plant and singing "You Are My Sunshine" with Chloe when Jason walked into the kitchen.

Chloe saw Jason first. Gladys didn't realize someone was in the house with them until Chloe started crying.

"What's wrong, sugar?" she asked, nearly dropping the watering can in her hand when she saw Jason standing there looking like a man on death row. "Jason? What are you doing here?"

Gladys kept Chloe behind her and glared at Jason though in truth the look in his eyes made her knees quake. He looked like death warmed over in his filthy clothes and oily hair, but it was the emptiness of his eyes that made Gladys want to take the baby and run in the opposite direction.

"No hello? Nice to see you? How've you been? Well, thanks for asking. Things have been a little rough to tell the truth." His voice cracked as if he'd been shouting at the top of his lungs at a rock concert before he arrived. He came toward her and she took a few steps back, weighing her exit strategy. Jason shook his head at her as if disappointed. "Aunt Gladys, you're hurting my feelings. That's plenty far." His voice hardened. "If you know what's good for you you'll stop."

Jason pulled a gun from the back of his grimy jeans' waistband and Gladys couldn't help the gasp that followed.

"Have you lost your mind, boy? You can't come in here and start waving a gun. You're frightening Chloe."

"Poor Chloe," he crooned and the sound sent a chill down Gladys's back. "Poor little daddy-less Chloe. The baby no one wants."

"Shut your mouth," Gladys said, anger vibrating through her stout body in spite of the danger that radiated from Jason's wasted body. "You hear me? Shut your filthy mouth before I slap you into next week. You've got no call to come in here and be nasty to this little girl."

"All right, all right," Jason snapped, waving Gladys down as if the sound of her voice grated on his strung-out nerves. "God, can't you take a joke? I was just kidding around."

"What do you want? Money? Fine. I'll get my purse, write you a check and you can get the hell out of my sight and never come back."

He shook his head and wiped at the thin rivulet of snot that trickled from his reddened nose and sucked back the rest. "Now you're really hurting my feelings, Auntie. I want my girls," he said. "Don't they miss me? Where are they?"

"Not here."

"Then where?"

Gladys switched tactics, delaying for time although she didn't know how she was going to get to the phone without him noticing. Somehow she didn't think he'd let her just walk to the phone and ring the sheriff.

"You look like hell. Let me guess, drugs?"

Jason scowled. "Shut up. Where's your purse?"

Petty little thief, she wanted to mutter but instead

moved past him to grab her purse on the table. Chloe's cries had turned to soft whimpers that pulled at Gladys's heart. She narrowed her gaze at Jason. "How much is it going to take to get you out of my life?"

His gaze turned shrewd. "How much you got?"

Gladys thought of her nest egg and narrowed her stare. "Enough. What's it going to take, Jason?"

"My girls…are they doing okay?" he asked. A disconsolate expression pulled his mouth into a grim line and he rubbed at his red-rimmed eyes with the flat of his palm while still gripping the gun. "I mean…do they ask about me?"

"No, they don't." Gladys stared at him coldly. "In fact, they're fine. Better since they've seen the last of you."

He looked at her. "What the hell are you talking about, old woman?"

"You've lost custody. There are consequences for neglect and abuse, Jason."

His stare hardened. "You old bitch."

"Foul-mouthed hooligan." She lifted her chin.

Jason lunged at Gladys but spooked Chloe instead and the toddler tried to bolt, attracting his attention. Gladys couldn't catch her fast enough but Jason could, the rage in his eyes scaring the life out of Gladys for Chloe's safety, not her own. "Chloe, no!" she screamed but Jason already had the baby in his grip.

Grabbing the toddler, he hoisted her in the air, the gun still in one hand, tipping her upside down until she screamed and Gladys squeezed tears from her eyes.

"Put her down," she ordered, trying for some semblance of authority but Jason merely laughed.

"Shut up, you old bag, and start writing that check. Besides—" he gave Chloe a shake "—I'm just playing. We used to do this all the time, didn't we, Chloe-baby? She loves it."

Gladys felt on the verge of begging, terrified for Chloe and of what Jason was capable of doing in his current mental state.

"I'm going to give you two seconds to put down that baby before I tear your head off."

The air rushed out of Gladys's lungs in undisguised relief as John and Renee came around the corner. There was murder in John's eyes and Gladys didn't feel sorry for Jason one bit for the beat-down that was coming his way.

RENEE WANTED TO RUSH JASON and rip Chloe out of his grasp but she was afraid he might drop the baby straight on her head out of spite. Fear kept her rooted but hatred flowed through her veins, thick and hot.

"Hey Rae…long time no see. Who's he?"

"Put. The. Baby. Down."

Jason slowly lowered Chloe but then dropped her the remaining distance and she fell. Gladys, closest to her, pulled the crying baby to her and put distance between them.

John stalked toward Jason until he raised the gun. "Ah, ah, ah. Remember who's holding the gun. That would be me, jackass, so before you go all John

McClane on me just remember I could shoot your nuts off."

"Jason, what's gotten into you?" Renee gasped. "Look at what you're doing. Why would you be so cruel? You didn't used to be like this."

Jason looked bleak. "Things change. Wives leave. Life sucks. Whatever, right?"

"You need help. How many nights have you been up?"

"Drug addict," John sneered under his breath and Renee swallowed hard, knowing that at this point Jason was capable of anything. This was not the man she'd known.

"You need help," Renee tried appealing to Jason's long-buried sense of self, hoping to touch that part she'd fallen in love with so long ago but the bile in her throat kept choking her. "Jason, you're in no shape to be around the girls…you have to know that. Do you want them to remember you like this?"

"My girls are gone. You've poisoned them against me," he said. A shadow passed over Jason's eyes and he wavered on his feet but the gun never changed position.

Renee shook her head. "You did that all on your own, Jason. I left the girls in your care and you neglected and abused them. And what you did to Chloe…"

"You're the one who left," Jason raged, spittle flying from his mouth. "Don't you dare go all righteous on me. You're no better, you lying drunk whore!"

Renee felt John tense beside her and she knew time was running out for any kind of peaceful resolution. A part of her didn't care. She hungered for violence for what he'd done to her girls but she was trying to find an ounce of mercy in her heart for the pathetic excuse of a man standing in front of her. Renee tried not to grit her teeth and dialed back the growl in her throat, knowing she needed to keep him talking somehow. "Why, Jason? Why would you try to hurt a baby?"

For a second Renee didn't think he'd answer. Finally, he rubbed at his eye and Renee almost thought she saw moisture but she couldn't be sure, as strung out as he was. "I stopped, okay? I felt like shit but you left me stuck with the kids and one of them wasn't even mine. I lost it. But she's fine, see? No harm no foul." At that, he chuckled as if he'd actually said something worth laughing about. It took great strength of will to keep her hands loose and not clenched in tight fists but she managed it until Chloe, reacting to the tension in the room, let loose with a high-pitched wail.

The ear-splitting decibel distracted Jason long enough for John, who was just waiting for the right moment, to make his move.

"Shut up!" Jason roared but as he turned back around he was met with five knuckles smashing into his nose. Blood splattered everywhere and Jason stumbled back screaming in pain. He tripped on his own feet and went down. John reared back and sent his booted foot right into his ribs. As Jason writhed in pain, Renee tried to drum up some sympathy for the man who was probably suffering from a broken nose and several cracked ribs but she felt nothing.

Her gaze traveled to John, breathing hard, big fists still clenched, and smiled. Holy hell. Suddenly amidst the bloody mayhem and the overall horrific nature of the last couple minutes…everything became blindingly clear. And for that she had Jason to thank. She let out a shaky breath as the adrenaline left her body in a rush and was replaced with something far more comforting.

Renee opened her mouth and…laughed.

"IN LIGHT OF THE EXTENUATING circumstances and the fact that your ex is in custody, I will forgive your missed court appearance."

Renee smiled. "Thank you, Your Honor."

Judge Lawrence Prescott II drew his paperwork together and then set it back down again, steepling his fingers in front of him. "From what I've read you've come a long way from the first day you stood before me. The children seem well-adjusted and ready to resume a relationship with you and you aren't carrying a chip on your shoulder any longer. I'm curious…what changed?"

Renee thought long and hard about that question. She let her gaze drift to John and his steady stare filled her with peace and happiness. Somehow she'd found a man who could love and protect three children who weren't his by blood, with everything in his power. She found a man who saw past her flaws and her issues and stood by her without enabling her to cling to bad patterns. What changed? For the first time in her life she fell in love with an honest-to-God good man. And you know what? She was going to marry that man. Not today. Maybe not even tomorrow. But someday. And she was going to learn to love the country.

And snow.

EPILOGUE

RENEE LOOKED STUNNING. John licked suddenly dry lips but couldn't pull his gaze from the vision standing before him. She was in a white halter dress that showed off creamy shoulders he longed to kiss and a nipped waist his hands itched to span.

His collar squeezed his neck but he didn't dare try to adjust it for he knew Evan would tease him mercilessly at the reception, or worse, knowing Evan, during the toast.

All three girls, miniature versions of their mother, stood to Renee's right while Evan's boys stood beside Evan to his left. Hot damn. John Murphy was finally getting married.

How'd he get so lucky? For as long as he lived, he'd remember the moment Renee walked up to him and said, "I'm in love with you, John Murphy, and if you have a problem with that you're just going to have to deal with it because I know you're in love with me, too." That was the best day of his life.

Then she'd grabbed him and laid a lip-lock on him that made bells go off in his head and his pants a bit tighter.

And that's what he loved about her. Well, one of the many things.

"Do you take this woman to be your lawfully wedded wife? To have and to hold till death do you part?" the minister asked, a smile wreathing his face as he regarded them kindly.

Renee gazed at him, her blue eyes shining like the ocean on a clear summer day, with a tremulous smile playing on her lips, and John knew there was nothing more he wanted in this life.

"I do," he answered solemnly.

Two words had never sounded so sweet.

* * * * *

*Celebrate 60 years of pure reading
pleasure with Harlequin!*

To commemorate the event, Harlequin Intrigue® is thrilled to invite you to the wedding of The Colby Agency's J. T. Baxley and his bride, Eve Mattson.

That is, of course, if J.T. can find the woman who left him at the altar. Considering he's a private investigator for one of the top agencies in the country—the best of the best—that shouldn't be a problem. The real setback is that his bride isn't who she appears to be…and her mysterious past has put them both in danger.

*Enjoy an exclusive glimpse of Debra Webb's latest
addition to*
THE COLBY AGENCY:
ELITE RECONNAISSANCE DIVISION

THE BRIDE'S SECRETS

Available August 2009 from Harlequin Intrigue®.

The dark figures on the dock were still firing. The bullets cutting through the surface of the water without the warning boom of shots told Eve they were using silencers.

That was to her benefit. Silencers decreased the accuracy of every shot and lessened the range.

She grabbed for the rocks. Scrambled through the darkness. Bumped her knee on a boulder. Cursed.

Burrowing into the waist-deep grass, she kept low and crawled forward. Faster. Pushed harder. Needed as much distance as possible.

Shots pinged on the rocks.

J.T. scrambled alongside her.

He was breathing hard.

They had to stay close to the ground until they reached the next row of warehouses. Even though she was relatively certain they were out of range at this point, she wasn't taking any risks. And she wasn't slowing down.

J.T. had to keep up.

The splat of a bullet hitting the ground next to Eve had her rolling left. Maybe they weren't completely out of range.

She bumped J.T. He grunted.

His injured arm. Dammit. She could apologize later.

Half a dozen more yards.

Almost in the clear.

As she reached the cover of the alley between the first two warehouses she tensed.

Silence.

No pings or splats.

She glanced back at the dock. Deserted.

Time to run.

Her car was parked another block down.

Pushing to her feet, she sprinted forward. The wet bag dragged at her shoulder. She ignored it.

By the time she reached the lot where her car was parked, she had dug the keys from her pocket and hit the fob. Six seconds later she was behind the wheel. She hit the ignition as J.T. collapsed into the passenger seat. Tires squealed as she spun out of the slot.

"What the hell did you do to me?"

From the corner of her eye she watched him shake his head in an attempt to clear it.

He would be pissed when she told him about the tranquilizer.

She'd needed him cooperative until she formulated a plan. A drug-induced state of unconsciousness had been the fastest and most efficient method to ensure his continued solidarity.

"I can't really talk right now." Eve weaved into the right lane as the street widened to four lanes. What she needed was traffic. It was Saturday night—shouldn't be that difficult to find as soon as they were out of the old warehouse district.

A glance in the rearview mirror warned that their unwanted company had caught up.

Sensing her tension, J.T. turned to peer over his left shoulder.

"I hope you have a plan B."

She shot him a look. "There's always plan G." Then she pulled the Glock out of her waistband.

Cutting the steering wheel left, she slid between two vehicles. Another veer to the right and she'd put several cars between hers and the enemy.

She was betting they wouldn't pull out the fire-power in the open like this, but a girl could never be too sure when it came to an unknown enemy.

Deep blending was the way to go.

Two traffic lights ahead the marquis of a movie theater provided exactly the opportunity she was looking for.

The digital numbers on the dash indicated it was just past midnight. Perfect timing. The late movie would be purging its audience into the crowd of teen-agers who liked hanging out in the parking lot.

She took a hard right onto the property that sported a twelve-screen theater, numerous fast-food hot spots and a chain superstore. Speeding across the lot, she selected a lane of parking slots. Pulling in as close to the theater entrance as possible, she shut off the engine and reached for her door.

"Let's go."

Thankfully he didn't argue.

Rounding the hood of her car, she shoved the Glock into her bag, then wrapped her arm around J.T.'s and merged into the crowd.

With her free hand she finger-combed her long hair. It was soaked, as were her clothes. The kids she bumped into noticed, gave her death-ray glares.

They just didn't know.

As she and J.T. moved in closer to the building, she grabbed a baseball cap from an innocent bystander. The crowd made it easy. The kid who owned the cap had made it even easier by stuffing the cap bill-first into his waistband at the small of his back.

Pushing through the loitering crowd, she made her way to the side of the building next to the main entrance. She pushed J.T. against the wall and dropped her bag to the ground. Peeled off her tee and let it fall.

His gaze instantly zeroed in on her breasts, where the cami she wore had glued to her skin like an extra layer. A zing of desire shot through her veins.

Not the time.

With a flick of her wrist she twisted her hair up and clamped the cap atop the blonde mass.

"They're coming," J.T. muttered as he gazed at some point beyond her.

"Yeah, I know." She planted her palms against the

wall on either side of him and leaned in. "Keep your eyes open. Let me know when they're inside."

Then she planted her lips on his.

* * * * *

Will J.T. and Eve be caught in the moment?
Or will Eve get the chance to reveal all of her
secrets?
Find out in
THE BRIDE'S SECRETS
by Debra Webb
Available August 2009 from Harlequin Intrigue®

We'll be spotlighting a different series every month throughout 2009 to celebrate our 60th anniversary.

LOOK FOR
HARLEQUIN INTRIGUE®
IN AUGUST!

To commemorate the event, Harlequin Intrigue® is thrilled to invite you to the wedding of the Colby Agency's J.T. Baxley and his bride, Eve Mattson.

Look for *Colby Agency: Elite Reconnaissance*

THE BRIDE'S SECRETS
BY DEBRA WEBB

Available August 2009

www.eHarlequin.com

HIBPA09

HARLEQUIN® *Romance®*

Welcome to the intensely emotional world of

MARGARET WAY

with

Cattle Baron: Nanny Needed

It's a media scandal! Flame-haired beauty
Amber Wyatt has gate-crashed her ex-fiancé's
glamorous society wedding. Groomsman
Cal McFarlane knows she's trouble, but when
Amber loses her job, the rugged cattle rancher
comes to the rescue. He needs a nanny, and
if it makes his baby nephew happy, he's
willing to play with fire....

*Available in August
wherever books are sold.*

www.eHarlequin.com

HRI760I

REQUEST YOUR FREE BOOKS!

2 FREE NOVELS PLUS 2 FREE GIFTS!

HARLEQUIN®

Super Romance®

Exciting, emotional, unexpected!

YES! Please send me 2 FREE Harlequin® Superromance® novels and my 2 FREE gifts (gifts are worth about $10). After receiving them, if I don't wish to receive any more books, I can return the shipping statement marked "cancel." If I don't cancel, I will receive 6 brand-new novels every month and be billed just $4.69 per book in the U.S. or $5.24 per book in Canada. That's a savings of close to 15% off the cover price! It's quite a bargain! Shipping and handling is just 50¢ per book*. I understand that accepting the 2 free books and gifts places me under no obligation to buy anything. I can always return a shipment and cancel at any time. Even if I never buy another book from Harlequin, the two free books and gifts are mine to keep forever.

135 HDN EYLG   336 HDN EYLS

Name _____ (PLEASE PRINT) _____

Address _____ Apt. # _____

City _____ State/Prov. _____ Zip/Postal Code _____

Signature (if under 18, a parent or guardian must sign)

Mail to the **Harlequin Reader Service:**
IN U.S.A.: P.O. Box 1867, Buffalo, NY 14240-1867
IN CANADA: P.O. Box 609, Fort Erie, Ontario L2A 5X3

Not valid to current subscribers of Harlequin Superromance books.

**Are you a current subscriber of Harlequin Superromance books
and want to receive the larger-print edition?
Call 1-800-873-8635 today!**

* Terms and prices subject to change without notice. Prices do not include applicable taxes. Sales tax applicable in N.Y. Canadian residents will be charged applicable provincial taxes and GST. Offer not valid in Quebec. This offer is limited to one order per household. All orders subject to approval. Credit or debit balances in a customer's account(s) may be offset by any other outstanding balance owed by or to the customer. Please allow 4 to 6 weeks for delivery. Offer available while quantities last.

Your Privacy: Harlequin is committed to protecting your privacy. Our Privacy Policy is available online at www.eHarlequin.com or upon request from the Reader Service. From time to time we make our lists of customers available to reputable third parties who may have a product or service of interest to you. If you would prefer we not share your name and address, please check here. ☐

HSR09R

You're invited to join our Tell Harlequin Reader Panel!

By joining our new reader panel you will:

- Receive Harlequin® books—they are FREE and yours to keep with no obligation to purchase anything!
- Participate in fun online surveys
- Exchange opinions and ideas with women just like you
- Have a say in our new book ideas and help us publish the best in women's fiction

In addition, you will have a chance to win great prizes and receive special gifts! See Web site for details. Some conditions apply. Space is limited.

To join, visit us at

www.TellHarlequin.com.

In 2009 Harlequin celebrates
60 years of pure reading pleasure!

We're marking this occasion by offering
16 **FREE** full books to download and read.

Visit

www.HarlequinCelebrates.com

to choose from a variety of
great romance stories
that are absolutely **FREE!**

(Total approximate retail value of $60)

We invite you to visit and share the Web site
with your friends, family
and anyone who enjoys reading.

COMING NEXT MONTH

Available August 11, 2009

#1578 WELCOME HOME, DADDY • Carrie Weaver
A Little Secret
An uncharacteristic one-night stand later, Annie Marsh knows her baby deserves a father he can count on. So she's ready to believe that the missing-in-action soldier who fathered her son is dead. Then the man shows up on her doorstep. Hard to say who's more shocked—Annie or reservist Drew Vincent....

#1579 BACK TO LUKE • Kathryn Shay
Riverdale, New York, is the last place Jayne Logan thought she'd end up. And Luke Corelli is the last man she thought she'd seek—given their past, a future is improbable. But with her life turning upside down, he is the one man she can trust... with her heart.

#1580 THE SECRET SIN • Darlene Gardner
Return to Indigo Springs
Annie Sublinski has never forgiven her teenaged self for putting her baby up for adoption. Still, she thinks she's moved on. Then she comes face-to-face not only with Ryan Whitmore—her daughter's father—but also with her daughter. Is unconditional love enough for three people to unite and become the family they deserve?

#1581 THE PROMISE HE MADE • Linda Style
Going Back
He said he'd come back. But when Serena Matlock's high school sweetheart Cole St. Germaine went to prison for a drunk driving accident, she never thought he'd keep that promise. He has. And now she has to find a way to tell him about the secret she's kept.

#1582 FIRST COME TWINS • Helen Brenna
An Island to Remember
Sophie Rousseau loved Noah Bennett when she was a teenager. But he couldn't wait to leave Mirabelle Island. Pregnant and alone, Sophie made a life for herself. Now Noah has come home, to discover a ready-made family. But he still has no plans to stay....

#1583 SAVE THE LAST DANCE • Roxanne Rustand
Everlasting Love
Jared Mathers was the perfect husband—his dedication to Kate and his unequivocal love for their daughter was the proof. Still, for Kate it wasn't enough. Now if fate gives them more time, she'll make sure she sets things right.

HSRCNMBPA0709